ECHO'S TALE

BURDEN OF THE TAIL

KHANYON G. JEROME

S.H.E. PUBLISHING, LLC

ECHO'S TALE | BURDEN OF THE TAIL
Copyright © 2021 by Khanyon G. Jerome

For information contact: Web: www.shepublishingllc.com | Email: info@shepublishingllc.com | Tel: 219.515.8032

Library of Congress Control Number: 2024935924

ISBN: 978-1-964061-07-8 (paperback)

Second Edition: April 2024

1 2 3 4 5 6 7 8 9 10

In Loving Memory
Kimberly Anne Davis
1967 - 2023

ACKNOWLEDGMENTS

I want to thank God and my supportive parents Arthur and Pamela Garey; without them, there would be no Echo's Tale, especially with how many times I had them read all my ideas.

To my lovely wife, Fawna Garey, thank you for allowing me to talk through my ideas with you. To my sister, Sahara Ware, she gave me the inspiration for the direction this book follows.

Here are the honorable mentions:

Dr. Jeffery Leech   Ashley McLean
Jason Conway   Elizabeth Conway
Kauri Ingram   Kimberly Davis
Mariah Lopez   Kayla Wright

Ultra (special mentions) You!

Without you, this book is nothing but words. You give this story meaning, and it is you that gives this tale life.

Thank you!

They say history repeats itself; that we are doomed to never learn from the past. If that is true, then my pain, my mistakes, and my sacrifices are eternal. Though that also means my love for you will echo throughout all time.

—Echo

PRELUDE

Tail End

Some stories change for various reasons, perhaps by culture or perhaps the reader was offended. Other stories are so gospel they never change no matter the stakes. Then there are some stories that are so compelling you need to only tell them once. With that being said, for my story, you may place it in any category you deem appropriate because I am choosing to tell you this tale only once.

Back in the end times of Railam, when it was still split between three Diatums, ruin befell this land when all the frothy hills of Gallium burned, and Nan Da'ruls beloved marble mountains shattered. Times were especially bleak when the mighty strength of Croix Ta'un surrendered their sanity.

For fourteen days, strong skies were overwrought and maroon. Clouds were agitated and thin as two creatures relentlessly fought one another—one of black with stars in his scales against one of absolute evil. The godly power of two dragons raged on as skies over the ruined Diatums quaked. The two dragons clawed, clashed, and bashed. Their flames met numerous times singeing the once snowcapped mountain below them.

The moment of the black dragon's defeat, his tail was ripped off clean; a ring of silence deafened the world as he fell to his death. What a day of tremendous sadness for a woman cloaked in cobalt; it was the first time she had ever grieved so zealously. Blue diamond tears fell from her cheeks as she held her fallen dragon in her arms. She sobbed as the body disintegrated like sand through her arms and fingers. She felt lost now, but it was not until she caught a glimpse of a tiny black tail no bigger than a wild carrot flailing underneath a pile of rubble. When she held it close to her heart, she could feel a tiny bit of life in this tiny bit of tail. She then made a vow, "I promise, Obsidian, I will protect you with every ounce of blood in my veins."

From that point on, she preserved the tail in a blue flame and hid away under the hills of Gallium and away from society. She was alone…

Well, so she thought; incidentally, she made a nest between two very feisty enemies: Diggle Pixies and Sath Spiders. As the woman cloaked in cobalt lived there, she grew fondly of the pixies and they to her. She also gained the respect of the Sath spiders stopping their generational war. But every night for a hundred years, she visited her fallen dragon begging for forgiveness—always leaving handfuls of diamond tears piled by the lantern that holds him.

"What was the cloaked woman's name?" asked by a pixie girl named Fonfon, ever so enthralled.

The beautiful caramel skinned woman looked down at Fonfon revealing her blue tipped braids that peeked from under her hooded cloak, gazing sorrowfully with sapphire eyes that matched the tenseness of her story.

"Her name is Echo, and this is my tale," she claimed.

Such pretentious words for Echo to think—to claim this story as her own and how brilliantly ignorant she must have felt, to find out that this tale she shares was anything but over. Because in the air, a graveled murmur spoke in a language only a spine chill could translate.

"No… It is mine!" Swift and unbeknownst, as the words turned a gruesome part of Echo's stomach, they slithered away to someone else's ears.

CHAPTER 1

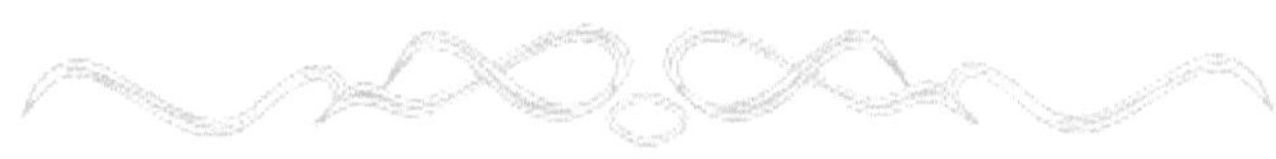

Dreams and Sunday Garments

One hundred and eighty-one years after Echo hid herself away, the people rebuilt their respective Diatums. But change was inevitable; noble families seized territory from their broken lords which caused chaos for a few years. To which by King Gallamar Fayos's iron fist, the land was quickly conquered. The first city in the middle of the country of Railam to emerge was Wallacgrum. Through stone and marble, Wallacgrum was built to become the leader of all other city dominions that sprouted thereafter: Agisshara, Facoom, Fahsoom, Salem, and Old Gallium.

Wallacgrum was a renaissance of resilience known for its vibrant emerald meadows and cherry blossom trees—a place where smiles and happiness felt almost tangible. The kingdom where the great King Christopher Fayos, son of late King Gallamar Fayos, shone his benevolent light upon all.

A light shone on most but not as much on a musty little treehouse just outside of the gates of Wallacgrum where a particular cotton-headed hermit by the name of Koldiar Neir settled—a Nubian sir who descended from Nuba Mandela and the first black man who stepped foot on Railam; even though Koldiar was not as dark or muscular as most Nubians could be, he was still distinctively Nubian. This was shown by his full lips and relatively thick eyebrows.

Despite being so young and being a hermit, he was quite capable of taking care of himself. He had to for most of his life due to a peculiar royal circumstance imposing him to live in solitude. This day was especially special for him because it marked Koldiar's nineteenth year past his birth, officially making him a man.

As a man, Koldiar was gifted with a dream, and this dream pulled him back in time to when he was a little boy. This was a time when he was still embraced by Wallacgrum and wanted nothing more but to be one of the king's personal Hayahs—a holy knight, sworn with the duties of guarding the royal family in the name of Jehovah. As a young boy, Koldiar's father was highly ranked, strong, and righteous both in duty and in stature—a great soldier but an even greater father.

Naturally, Koldiar and the Princess Ismiellia met, and she quickly became his closest and only friend. The two often snuck around the castle playing together and frolicking in the royal garden pretending to save one another from evil dragons. Koldiar dreamt of these lovely memories every night, but as you might know, all good things come to an end. No longer sure if this was a dream, memory, or a prophecy, all he could recall was he was running through the garden with Ismiellia.

The turn for the worst began on a peaceful afternoon in one of Wallacgrum's many luscious meadows where Koldiar and Princess Ismiellia often laid and watched the clouds. They would sit together on the tall soft grass blissfully watching as billowy clouds rolled above them with such wonder. Thunder boisterously shook the sky; dark clouds, rain, and lightning quickly rolled in after. The children looked at each other and reluctantly agreed to go back inside, but as they turned around, they found themselves face-to-face with a ravenous dire wolf threatening their lives. As if second nature, Koldiar pulled Ismiellia behind him and stared this hair raised wolf down with equal intent to kill. The snarling dire wolf was more than ready to rip them both to shreds when suddenly, something deep down inside of Koldiar's subconscious awakened. His face began to mirror the wolf; his nails and teeth grew larger and sharper.

The tension was so fragile a heartbeat could almost shatter it. The anticipation became too unbearable for Ismiellia; her body flinched without her permission. The wolf then pounced; Koldiar drew his hand back, and with all his might, he swiped with a gusty blow. The attack blew the creature into a perching bolder breaking its neck and leaving it lifeless. Its unresponsive body tumbled behind the bolder. Koldiar felt confused and exhilarated until he turned around to see Ismiellia holding her face with blood seeping between her fingers. He had unintentionally gashed her face; horrified, Koldiar tried to apologize, but the shock and shame he had muzzled his intent to speak. By the time the shock wore off, it was too late to say anything. Six royal guards rushed over and naturally flocked toward Princess Ismiellia, asking her, "Princess! Princess! What happened?

Who did this to you?"

She glared at Koldiar and pointed. She did not say a word as they all looked at him with vindicating eyes. She blamed him… They all blamed him.

"No! I did not mean to! I-It was the wolf, h-he did it! Please… no. Ismi, no! You have to believe me!"

Koldiar begged so hard that tears began to roll down his cheek, but the guards still walked toward him slowly drawing their swords. The closer they walked, the darker his surroundings became until he was alone standing in complete darkness. Koldiar tried to scream, but in that type of darkness, the only thing that could be heard was the thump of his rapidly beating heart. Sounding like someone was beating a large drum as hard as they could into his ear. He could also hear the slimy gulp of his own saliva and the bubbling groans of his digesting belly. Suddenly, everything stopped; he could no longer hear nor see. Out of the darkness, a blue flame ignited on top of the white podium with something that resembled a small black tail placed inside it. Before him appeared a dragon the size of four horses, graciously coiled around the podium and in deep slumber.

It's not a particularly mean looking dragon nor an ugly dragon by any means; in fact, it probably was the most beautiful and peaceful creature he had ever seen—blue like the summer sky but also glittery like refined diamonds. Its scales were as if crystals had been slicked down its lanky body covering its deep blue skin. Koldiar was amazed by how the scales on its wings looked almost like crystalized feathers as they tucked beneath each other. However, after too long of staring in awe, the dragon woke up and noticed him. A fearsome roar bellowed from the angry dragon, a terrifying sound as if three dragons were roaring.

The shock from the boisterous dragon and the gush of cold water jolted Koldiar awake, heavily panting as he gathered his thoughts and pulled himself together. Koldiar looked up and noticed that his poorly built roof had caved in due to the weakening force of rainwater collected throughout the night.

Groaning, as he pulled himself out of his drenched straw bed and after inspection of the gaping hole, he said to himself, "Well, I guess it is going to be one of those days…" Koldiar further groaned, realizing he had to fix his roof then even louder because had to go to town. Nevertheless, he grabbed his best "Sunday go to market" clothes from the slightly damp sack underneath his bed. The sack consisted of two brown sandals so mildewed they ripped when he strapped them on an olive-green tunic he found on the side of the road; he could have sworn it was originally white but put it on all the same. Lastly, he had a pair of black trousers that cuffed at his ankles, not because they were conveniently in style but because they were that old. Although he might deem his attire appropriate for going out, any civilized person would view him as simply dingy. Dingy might be the only word to describe this poor man's tattered apparel. He dressed himself without any other preparations and climbed down from his treehouse. Secluded from the rest of the townsfolk, he walked a long way out of his allotted woods and toward the morning light peaking between drooping branches.

Along his path, a sparkle of post rain dew touched every blade of grass, even the leafless willow trees were drenched. The air was filled with a scent of faint ginger, accompanied by a thick dung ferret manure undertone, from the mud. Koldiar loved to squish through the patches of mud and grass with his bare feet; he was rather simple that way because he liked this feeling a lot more than he should have.

Although he was prepared to get only what he needed and go back home, however, something more exciting would become of his life.

It had been years since Koldiar had been in town, so he hardly recognized any landmarks or the people. Everything seemed so vibrant and different. It was all much larger than he remembered, the buildings especially; most of the homes he passed became more frequent and were most often symmetrical with low-pitched, hipped tiled roofs, and broad boxed-in eaves. Koldiar was confused as to why there were miniature houses connected to the bigger house. He just thought to himself, "Hmm, times must be hard for people to have to live together. Good thing I have my own house."

Koldiar was in awe at how each building was more lavish than the last even though he pitied the poor families who had to live together. He could still appreciate that they were garnished with a plethora of flowers and ribbons. In hindsight, anything would have been more lavish than the tree shack he calls home. Nevertheless, his boyish wonder and amazement distracted him—so much so that the supplies he intended to get were no longer that crucial. When he reached the inner city, he had all but forgotten about why he was there in the first place.

The buildings were monumental with impossible dome shaped roofs. Koldiar loved walking under the façade arches and around segmental columns of Wallacgrum's grand library, undoubtedly gathering a few unsavory glances. It appeared that everything was made of marble aside from the parapets of stone surrounding the city and the castle where King Fayos resided. Koldiar stayed away from that castle as far as he could; instead, he was distracted by music, jugglers, and fire eating acts captivating all the city folk.

Koldiar could not help but notice there were more than just humans that lived here; now there were Cedars, Dwarves, Elves, and Demilings all celebrating together. But like a slippery snake, a smelly smell crept up upon him, twisting and turning through the crowd and filled his nostrils with curiosity.

"What is this meaty smell?" he asked the little girl next to him. "What? That? That is the Malomeak stand."

"Malomeak?"

"Yeah, it is a roasted ball of salted Buke meat with sweet brown gravy in the middle. It is really quite good. The stand's right over there behind the stage," she said, pointing to the stand before becoming utterly distracted by the jugglers setting his juggling spheres on fire. Koldiar's body moved on its own straight for the food stand.

When out of a dusty parting between two buildings, a dirty old beggar man staggered out courting his attention saying, "Boy, boy, boy, I feel something very special coming from you!"

At this time, Koldiar probably should have walked away, especially when he spotted the crazed look in the beggar man's eyes.

"Can I have some silver?" the man asked.

He then grabbed Koldiar's hand to read his future within the lines. "Yes! Great things are coming your way, my boy! Great, great love, beautiful love but first you must find her, and when you find her, protect her! Can I have some silver now?" He then grabbed the other hand, and his face contorted, and his eyes widened as he said, "Let us see… What… Whaaaat eeevvviiillll! You, you are a monster! You must be killed! Quick, everyone! Kill him before we all get killed ourselves!" He yelled to all the festival people. "This boy is evil! Hide your kids! Hide your wives! Hide your husbands! He is going to kill us all!"

Koldiar was at a loss, and for a moment, he was a bit worried about what the people would do. That is until he saw that no one was paying him any mind; in fact, many of them rolled their eyes at him. Koldiar just got as far away from this man as possible despite how calm everyone seemed. Koldiar was a bit agitated because those Malomeak balls started smelling appetizing, but because of that man's fishy breath, he thoroughly lost his appetite. However, his boyish curiosity stirred once again and immediately saw something else that allured more his attention causing him to wander away.

CHAPTER 2

Dreams and Decisions

As Koldiar walked through alleys and over marble bridges, he thought maybe he would be able to see King Fayos again and possibly earn his place within his ranks. He could not help but remember how King Fayos's presence was large, sturdy, and bigger than life—just like the wall that protected his kingdom—also, how he looked up to this dark-skinned Nubian king for giving him the special task of upkeeping the forest.

Everyone knew that even from a young age, King Fayos was referred to as a god among men, and Koldiar was no different. From his enjoyment in shared folly, to his stoic seriousness when angered, Fayos was most thoroughly revered or feared if there was ever an occasion that infuriated this otherwise jolly man.

For instance, if you did not much care for him (though everyone usually did), you could not help but respect him on sight alone. He was a brilliant man with extraordinary tactical sense that once convinced an army of giga trolls that instead of invading the kingdom and causing war, Wallacgrum was the only thing protecting them from the sun that wanted to burn them alive. Although untrue, it was not readily apparent to the trolls as they lack a specific type of intelligence. This was only one example of how clever King Fayos was, but despite his cleverness, he could not think himself healthy.

As for Koldiar, he was unaware that King Fayos had even come down with an illness until he kept overhearing the news from the townsfolk. Cliphus fever was what they called it, also known as the black cough, had taken a toll on the king's fragile body. It was also known as the single-symptom slayer; this insidious plague only reared its ugly head every fifty years. If you were hapless enough to contract it, you would find yourself uncontrollably spewing black metallic blood. Woefully, the king was all too aware of this rancorous virus and how it always seemed to claim a handful of noblemen in its wake. Sadly enough, King Fayos's blood was rotting from the inside and that he would undoubtedly perish soon.

News had been spreading for weeks that King Fayos had begun looking weaker as he would expel enormous amounts of rotted blood in private and would continue to hack and wheeze unintentionally in the middle of ceremonies, dinners, and speeches. Stories were also being told that nights for the poor king were far more tortuous as most of them seemed to be spent doing everything other than sleeping, undoubtedly in fear of his soul-wrenching nightmares that would leave him in a cold sweat—nightmares you could tell were filled with despair and darkness just by the gossip.

Although everyone could tell how fearful the once almighty king was, he still had a demeanor to uphold—strong enough to show himself to be dignified and that he was the fearless leader he was widely known to be. For he feared no one would be safe without him. Perhaps he was a bit arrogant with his views, but there was no doubt he loved his kingdom and feared for his people.

Fortunately, King Fayos had at least one minor pause in despair, and it was the weeklong festival Koldiar had walked through. Two mornings before Koldiar's arrival into the city, all the townsfolk banded together and formed a line from the grand hall doors stretching all the way to the town's circle, spending the early part of the week presenting their best items to cheer their king up. Whether their gifts be milk, meat, metal, or fine fabrics, everything was appreciated.

The first people in this grandiose line was a small elderly woman and her anxious grandson, ready to give three dozen of their best purple beckled speckled eggs. They knew very well King Fayos had an unusual habit of eating eggs raw, and they thought the rarely laid speckled eggs would be a nice treat for him. King Fayos graciously accepted the little boy's large basket that was propped atop his head. "Thank you, young sir, and thank you, ma'am. These are an absolute treat!" the king expressed as his guards gathered the eggs from the nervous little boy that bowed his head.

"You are welcome, Your Majesty!" he shouted with a shrill yet boisterous tone.

"Boy, there is no need to be nervous. Look here, take this," Fayos said in a deep and powerful tone. He grabbed a very large gold coin from his pocket and flicked it into the tiny hands of the very little boy. "Remember, when you get nervous again, just squeeze that coin…then when you do not need it to be brave anymore, go buy you and your lovely grandmother something sweet."

Both the little boy and his grandmother walked away smiling and blushing, happy in many ways. Behind them was a scholarly gentleman with a greenish tent to his leathery white skin holding a massive bundle of scrolls, nearly dropping all of them as he bowed before the king.

"Heh, I apologize, Your Majesty… I, Thespis Oltrage, have brought you the only thing I have to give. All my greatest poems and plays, take them, please! Bring honor to my craft!"

This man was so profoundly serious about his poems King Fayos felt he had no choice but to graciously accept.

"It is my honor, My Lord, I pray you will find deeper meaning in my extraordinary poems. Thus, I pray you relish the true intent in my words as I have molded them into divine existence as there can be no modesty in my eyes," Thespis insisted, inching away bowing repeatedly until he left the king's sight.

The day ended in a drunken stupor as all the townsfolk feasted and drank in the streets. Unfortunately, while fireworks exploded in the dusk sky, King Fayos could not enjoy the moment and was forced to watch from his balcony. He was plagued by the black cough as his seemingly cursed mortal body betrayed him in weakness. On the verge of passing out, he staggered through the corridor leading to his chambers. Halfway through his corridor, his unsteady gait worsened until crash! Fayos clamored to the floor, coughing hysterically; black blood stained his hands and blouse. As he struggled to stand, his legs betrayed him too. Knocking over one of his end tables, King Fayos's daughter Princess Ismiellia caught him just as he submitted to the floor.

Ismiellia was an orphan of no royal blood when both King Fayos and his late wife, Queen Mara Fayos, chose to adopt her as a baby. She was a fair-skinned human with soft hazel eyes and dark raven hair; in other words, she was Wavian, a descendant of Wavya Hasnan. Though she is not of noble blood, by royal decree by the great King Fayos, she would be a suitable successor to the throne. This princess orphan was shamed by the scar she tried to conceal on her bottom left cheek but that motivated her to protect anyone who needed her; however, at this point in her life, her father was that person who needed her the most.

"No, no, come on, Father, we cannot sleep here," she said. "Heh, but the floor there looks so comfortable," Fayos said, joking and coughing at the same time.

"Father...I told you that you need to be resting!" she insisted in a calm reassuring tone.

"The people need to know that their king is still strong, or else chaos may break loose. I have to be 'king,' as is my duty. It is honestly out of my hands," he asserted.

"I would rather the world burn than to lose you," she said. "Oh, Ismi...I promise I will never leave you."

However, that was a promise King Fayos knew was impossible to keep.

"You can leave. I am fine now. I need a moment to pray." "Okay, Father. I will send someone to check on you in a bit."

King Fayos humbled himself as he kneeled at his bedside. He then spoke his prayer aloud to make sure God heard him.

"Jehovah-Rapha, my prayers are out to you. Your Grace, please grant me more time if being cured is no option. Lord, I am desperate. I wish not for a day...not even for another hour...but for five more minutes. Only five minutes, and if you allow it, please grant me five more. This kingdom needs me, my daughter needs me! Lord, she is not ready for this kingdom...not just yet. So please grant me five minutes until she is. Elohim, El Shaddai, let your will be done."

Following that evening, King Fayos laid in his bed unable to sleep due to his usual agony. He figured a bit of light reading may help him rest a bit easier than the previous tossing and turning. So he grabbed one of Thespis's poems from his nightstand and began to read. Inside this black leather back scroll read, "Tail of young, and a tail of old, a tail shadowed, and a tail brightened. Two tails quarreling through history while burdened with so much pain. The black tail ended by the fray, though its life is gone, its power still remains."

Somehow those words eased the king asleep as though a villain had intentionally drugged him. In his slumber, he dreamt a dream unlike any other. In an imaginary land where an almighty king can be as vulnerable as a babe. His new vision exhibited something that filled the king with awe-inspiring hope and laid the foundation for the rest of his tale.

Rays of warm glistening light kissed the kings face, awaking him from his dream. It was almost like the sun knew the morning was going to be good—preposterous, really, as if the sun had a consciousness or the magical ability to do such an amazing task—and quite laughable, indeed you would not believe how correct the sun was. King Fayos was full of energy and uncomfortably joyful despite having to deal with the unbearable pain of the black cough that did not seem to bother him much anymore; in fact, the paleness in his face seemed to have lessened.

That night, he had another dream, but this time, it was more vivid than the last. The more he daydreamed about his new dreams, the more the king appeared optimistic that Jehovah had absolutely heard his prayer. He started trusting this dream to be a fiction, an obtainable truth. Therefore, he let down his royal guard and paced up and down his corridors telling anyone that had a moment of time about his incredible life-altering dream. Even if they did not have the time of day, he was not above negating whatever occupied their time otherwise. As king, though, no one would dare refuse or ignore him except for his daughter, of course. She thought it foolish that a king would put so much excitement and hope into an inauspicious fable.

However, he cared little of what she thought, and to everyone else, he explained his dream as such.

"There I sat alone in my throne room. It was so cold even the candles were smothered out by the chill. Dark and stormy, I could feel every soul in my kingdom approaching to watch me struggle for the last bit of air I clung to. I felt like a child again, clenching their leaving mother's leg, but my grip was slipping. Then three loud clangs sounded at the castle gate. Clang! The first one shook the castle, cracking the stone floor and shattering every window. All the while, I could hear children laughing and chanting, 'Tail of young, tail of old, tail of dark, tail of bright.

A tail of dark! A tail of bright! A tail of death!' nothing I did could muffle the taunting children as they got louder and louder, ringing my ears.

"Clang! The second one summoned six chains from the shadows binding my person, but this time, I could hear rabid dogs barking as though they were right next to me snapping at my ears. Clang! The last clang morphed the throne room doors into sand that cascaded down to reveal warriors, townspeople, and other kings. I knew that they were there to pilfer everything I had built! The ceiling then turned to sand, and as sand rained down on me, a ferocious gust of wind rolled in. A daunting black yet beautiful dragon appeared before me, and when I really looked at it, I was confused by how truly black it was. Wonder and excitement could not begin to describe its deepness. It was captivating… Yes! It was captivating! It was hard to look at him, but what I do remember were his scales—scales that were speckled like the starry night sky. Its colossal wings overfilled the room's capacity as if his wings were part of the shadows.

"The black dragon had come to my rescue. He protected me! He fought tooth and nail against all the kings and townsmen trying to kill me. Alas, the beast was overwhelmed. A large arrow pierced his heart, and he fell to the ground. Even though the dragon was defeated, he continued to try and protect me. Before the dragon submitted to the inevitable and the arrow fully took his life, he ripped off the tip of his tail and tossed it to my feet. His voice, like thunder, exclaimed, 'My power is yours for the taking if you only consume it.' After hearing those words, I summoned the strength and broke the chains that bound me. I retrieved the speckled tail at once and bit into it. Energy whelmed up inside of me. I felt stronger than ever. I felt healthy. I felt powerful!

"People could now see me again and understand that I am stronger than I once was. With the ferocious power of a dragon coursing through my veins, 'I am invincible!' I said.

"I demanded that the other kings bow first, to which they did, and their people bowed as well! I was a king to the kings now as I rose above the room, above all those who thought me frail, who thought me weak!

"In the distance, I could faintly hear a cry, then across my back, I felt an icy sensation as a blue flame then consumed my body. It forced me to regurgitate the tail thus robbing me of all my energy and power. It left me painfully feeble as I drop into darkness. When the dream faded into black, the blue flames covered the tail and shot off into the distance, waking me up."

The following day, the dream, and the words "Its power still remains" were all that King Fayos thought about and caused him to become obsessed. By the time Koldiar entered the city, everyone in the kingdom knew about that dream that had now firmly embedded itself into King Fayos's existence—so much so he had already written a decree before the sun rose. He was now willing to use all his power to get the tail back and make his dream a reality. He refused to rest until someone, anyone, acquired his dragon's tail.

CHAPTER 3

Some Kingsman

Meanwhile, a shameful deal was in progress as Koldiar still wandered the city of Wallacgrum. Not far from him, in a murky alley in the Bogus district, two men met. Both figures dawned in shrouded hoods covering their faces. The one on the left was six-foot tall and terrifyingly malnourished, by how his black shroud draped his body, like a child underneath a bedsheet. This man, for the sake of the story and the fact that no one really remembers his name, shall be called Victor Stow, a weasel of a man that made his profit from stealing anything that was not nailed to the floor. Somehow, he was able to procure a job guarding the king's treasure. As you are all probably thinking, how does a thief like that secure a royal job? I can only assume powerful magic was involved— dark magic that forcibly warps a man's mind without their consent… or he was just a remarkable liar.

As for the second man, he wore a white shroud seamed with gold trimmings. This man was not much shorter than the first. The only real difference was the fact that he was on the plumper end of the spectrum— not too overweight but just plump enough to know that he has never skipped a meal or dessert if he was ever so inclined. This slightly stout man, if you can even call him such a thing, was a short-horned Demiling. Which is, if you did not know your Railam history, is an ancient, cursed variant of humans considered Creeps. With red tinted skin and horns that varied in size, but at this point in history they are a race in their own right. Despite mildly resembling demons, most of them, if not all, do not act as such a creature. Having more or less the same tendencies of a straightforward human, this despicable Demiling was named Orien Fike.

"Were you able to acquire my box, Victor?" asked Orien. "Only barely but yes," Victor said while pulling a little gold box out of his bag. "Be careful with it! It will force you into lucid sleep." Victor advised before completing their transaction by swapping the golden box for the sack of eighty gold pieces.

"Mmm, good," Orien said, admiring his prize. "Oh, before I leave," Orien continued, "do you have any interesting information for me?"

"I do actually, apparently, the king wants a dragon's tail, and apparently, he is willing to give anything for it. I was able to swap out the decree with a decoy, so only I know where the possible location is. I will sell it for another eighty pieces." Orien looked at Victor intrigued as a heinous idea popped into his head.

Orien opened the box and out danced the most enchanting melody radiating from Orien's hands like smooth warm fire.

Victor drowsily says, "Wait, what are you doing, you idiot! Orien! We…had…a…deal…" Victor melted to the floor unconscious.

Orien crouched down, picking out two globs of wax from his ears, saying, "See, what you have to understand is eighty gold pieces was too expensive."

Orien then scavenged through Victor's pockets taking all his gold back and a bit of Victor's silver too. He also took everything Victor had along with the scroll that he spoke of. After he gathered all "his" things, he headed farther into town to the local tavern in order to meet up with his partner in crime.

This particular tavern was famous or rather infamous for being the scummiest bar in Wallacgrum called the Flattened Beak. Honestly, looking inside this less-than-tolerable dwelling, it came to no surprise that no one takes any pride in its care. Orien may be, could be, was the type of scoundrel that would burn down a church before he would ever pay back money owed, but he did have more standards than to be in a place like this.

Practically, all the people in Wallacgrum had high standards and took decorating to an obsessive level. Even the cemeteries rival King Fayos's royal garden. So when others refused to acknowledge or compliment their efforts, it was a sloppy slap in the face. The people of Wallacgrum undoubtedly insult very easily. More specifically, shop owners or staff wanted to hear the phrase "nice a gully gove!" the moment you walk through the door. Anything less is an insult to the highest regard.

To reiterate, this tavern was not nice nor was it a gully gove in the slightest. Orien did not feel the tavern was deserving of a compliment. Luckily enough, the workers there knew how much of a rubbish dump the Flattened Beak was, so they were callused to unhappy customers. Nevertheless, he sat down at the bar next to his friend and ordered a pint of mead. There, next to Orien, was his partner and best friend—a gnome, just as money hungry as his counterpart— Syric Olen, proficient in thievery and prestidigitation. This fellow had a slight disposition, though; being a gnome, he was highly quick to temper—that is, if anyone were to ever think of acknowledging his height or the lack thereof.

They both drank and joked about how Orien obtained the box and how angry Victor must have been. They also spoke of all the possibilities for the box and mildly bickered about who was going to use it first for a task of thievery. Incidentally, they changed the topic when Syric drunkenly slipped out of his chair.

"Ha ha. Are you okay, my friend?" Orien inquired before pulling out the scroll. "I grabbed this scroll too. Apparently, the king wants people to look for a tail."

"A tail?" Syric replied, pulling himself back into his seat.

"Yes, and one from a dragon no less," he said while handing over the scroll.

"Hmm...I don't like it. How do we even know this is real? And even if it is, how do we get it? I have no idea how to kill a dragon, do you?" Syric asked.

"Upon many topics, just because you say 'don't' does not mean the word will catch on. It just makes you sound ignorant. Secondly, just think of the money we stand to make!"

"Hey! I said nothing when you tried to sell feet cloth for sandals even though we both knew it was a stupid idea!"

Sitting close to Orien and Syric, an old scruffy wornout gentleman could not help but to eavesdrop on all of their bickering and boisterous talking. Annoyed as he was at first, especially with Syric's unnecessarily loud speaking voice, their conversation did pique his interest.

Eventually, he was compelled to join them by saying, "The little one is correct. Do not bother trying to find it. You are either going to be disappointed or get yourselves killed."

"Little one?" Syric took a moment to look at him, then to Orien, and then back at him. He could not believe the blatant audacity this man had. Therefore, to calm the bubbling anger within himself, he chocked it up to the old man being drunk.

"Anyway, dragons are not real. Do you know anyone that has ever seen one before…no, and there is a reason for tha—"

Again, the old man pushed his luck by cutting Syric off midsentence.

"Dragons are very real but very hard to find. There is a reason not many people have seen one. There was a class in the school of mastery that teaches all there is to know about those dangerous creatures, which is not very much—"

"And you took this class?" Syric scoffed.

The old man then mumbled his reply into his wooden mug.

"What?" Syric shouted.

"I taught it! For thirty years! All down the drain and for what? To sit here drunk, explaining myself to some gnome," he said before guzzling down the rest of his drink.

With a timely queued hiccup, he slapped two silver pieces on the bar top and attempted to hobble his way out of the tavern.

However, before he could completely walk away, he overheard Orien say to Syric, "Hmm, okay…anyway, apparently, just a piece of the dragon tail is needed upon delivery, and he is willing to pay as much as we want for it."

In the most perfect fluid motion, the old man turned around and introduced himself.

"My apologies, gentlemen, I was so impolite. Let me buy you a drink. Bartender! Two pints over here!" Leaving no room to breathe, the old man continued, "Allow me to introduce myself. I am professor Fuzen Waykin, former Wizard of the Royal Mystic Court! I am at your service." Fuzen graciously bowed.

"Service yourself and go away," said Syric even though Fuzen ignored him and spoke only to Orien.

"If you are going to go after a dragon, you are going to need more than a feisty sprite for help."

"You bring a very good point. How about I cut you in for eighty," Orien negotiated.

"Oh no, you are too generous. Eighty percent is way too much.

I would settle for sixty-five," Fuzen excitedly negotiated.

"Oh, I am sorry for the confusion. It is eighty pieces to be a part of our crew and twenty-five percent for your cut."

"You want me to pay you to help you?" Fuzen scoffed, baffled by his audacity.

"Hmm, eighty gold," Orien said, holding out his hand waiting for the gold.

"I only have forty on me...," Fuzen said, confused, and though he had not done any work yet, he already felt cheated.

"All right, seventy then! My final offer." Orien leaned back on the bar, crossing his arms, refusing to cheapen his price any further.

"You understand not. Forty pieces is all I have."

"Hmm...okay, I will make you a deal. I want that..." Orien shifted his gaze to Fuzen's staff.

"Want what?" Fuzen said, looking concerned. "Your walking stick."

"My staff?"

"Yeah, I want your walking stick."

"No?" Fuzen said, highly unsure of Orien's sanity.

"Well then, sorry, wizard. I think our group has reached its limit—" Orien said, closing business by folding his arm.

"How about this, after we finish, I will provide you with a much nicer…walking stick, something with jewels!" Fuzen suggested.

"I do like jewels…," Orien muttered.

Syric chimed in, "No no! We don't need you nor do we want you." He was standing on his stool, looking Fuzen dead in his eyes.

Fuzen tapped him on the forehead and made a hiss sound, freezing him in ice.

Orien jumped to his feet, excited, and impressed by such magical mastery Fuzen demonstrated.

"Deal!" he said, shaking Fuzen's hand and putting his arm around his shoulders.

"Fuzen, was it? My name is Orien Fike. Follow me to a place where we can really plot."

Before walking out, they realized they almost forgot about Syric—that is, before Syric let out a high-pitched whine for help.

Orien pointed at the frozen gnome while saying to Fuzen, "Yeah, we actually kind of need him."

"Very well," Fuzen reluctantly sighed.

He then proceeded to tap Syric's forehead once more, exhaling vapors, melting the ice away.

Embarrassed and able to move freely, Syric walked to Orien, saying, "You know I could kill him right!? With the same spell Zetho the great used to defeat the orc army! But I don't want to kill everyone here. Also, it does seem like he is more useful alive, so I suppose he can come…"

Poor Syric walked past them, hoping no one saw or would acknowledge what had just happened. As he began to walk through the tavern threshold, a homeless man hurled past the door entrance, cutting Syric off, the same mad homeless man that troubled Koldiar for a hand reading earlier that morning. The guys were so baffled they could not help but to peek outside the door. All their heads were stacked one above the other peeking toward the direction the body came from. That is where they saw Koldiar frozen in fear, heavily panting.

Confidently enough, Orien believed he could profit off this situation. Therefore, he took the initiative and walked up to Koldiar as Syric and Fuzen loosely followed behind.

Just as Orien began to introduce himself, Koldiar blurted out,

"Sorry…I am so sorry I did not mean to…he was…and I was…he jumped on top of me! And…and…" Koldiar was frantic!

"Whoa, whoa! I did not ask for your whole life story," Orien said, almost pushing Koldiar off him.

Before Koldiar could reply, twelve guards arrived with Victor Stow leading the front line.

"There he is. Get him!" Victor Stow shouted.

By that point, everyone, even innocent bystanders, had the instinct to scatter.

Orien, with his head turned, said, "Hey, kid, I have a proposition for you. Just follow us…"

When Orien looked back for a response, Koldiar had already started running as if his back were on fire. Orien did not waste time either, nor did Fuzen or Syric. They all instinctively followed behind Koldiar.

The guards charged as Koldiar, Orien, Fuzen, and Syric ran as fast as they could. They swore they could feel the tips of the guards' swords grazing their backs as they caught up. Surely, slowing down even for a second would spell death…or worse, their assets being seized. Koldiar had no clue where he was going; all he knew was that he needed to be further than everyone else. Foolishly, Koldiar looked back at his pursuers, and with an awkward crash, he ran into a slaughterhouse hog that escaped for its owner's pin, thrashing his face on the stone floor.

Fuzen developed a quick plan; he gripped the staff attached to his back and made the sound "Fuhoo!" He then drew a circle on the ground with the top end of his staff. What followed after created an enormous dust cloud that engulfed the entire street. Luckily, in that brief moment, Syric was able to place Koldiar on his tiny shoulders and carry him off to safety. Slick and sly, the four of them managed to slip away from the guards, unseen.

CHAPTER 4

A Forceful Journey

AFTER AWAKING FROM AN UNTIMELY HOG ACCIDENT, Koldiar frantically twisted and flailed only to find himself constricted. He was being manhandled by a gnome!—a very powerful one at that. Still groggy, Koldiar wanted nothing more than to be unhanded as any normal person would if they found themselves carried against their will. However, in a panic, to avoid unwanted attention, Fuzen whacked Koldiar on the head with his staff, knocking him out for the second time.

While unconscious, Koldiar had another dream, but this time, it started where the last dream left off. He was standing in front of the magnificently majestic blue crystal dragon after it echoed its last roar. It lied down coiling itself back around its white pedestal, paying no mind to Koldiar and forgetting his existence. On top the tower like pedestal, the blue flame grew larger as the dragon slept. The larger the flame grew so did Koldiar's compulsion to reach into the flame. With a mixture of curiosity and terror, he crept closer, becoming so bold as to climb over the sleeping dragon. However, no matter how gently Koldiar stepped, he could hear every jewelry-like crackle within its scales.

While staggering through the dragon's scales, Koldiar started to feel a tiny bit of warmth radiating from the fire up top. He leapt from the sleeping dragon to the trunk of the pedestal, grabbing onto a protruding engraved D. Koldiar's determination gave him the motivation to climb higher. He clasped upon the base of the E of the protruding word let above him and then pushed harder to scale the H above that. Finally, triumphing on top of the O that came next. He failed to notice that the engraved letters he frivolously climbed up was actually a warning that stated, "do not let him out."

Upon reaching the top, Koldiar felt a cold warmth that sent icy chills down his spine. There before him was a blue flame bigger than his treehouse, and it seemed too tantalizing not to reach into it. The flame split open as if it were a cage, inviting him inside. Koldiar soon realized that this fire was in fact a cage for inside was a tail. This tail was as black as obsidian, freckled with white specks making it look like the night sky.

Koldiar's mouth was dry from anticipation, yet his finger danced with excitement. Barely grazing the tail with his dirty chipped fingernail, the fire closed and engulfed his whole arm. The flame rapidly faded from blue to black. He was terrified and began to pull and tug his arm, but he was hopelessly stuck. He desperately tried to scream, but no sound left his lungs.

Koldiar struggled as the dragon lifted its head, noticing him with ferocious sapphire eyes. As young bold hermit noticed the dragon gazing at him, he could not help to feel overwhelmed by the dragon's piercing blue eyes. Although filled with snarling anger, there were tears that rolled down one side of its face as well.

Like a volcano of pain and rage, she roared in what sounded like an echoing scream. "Leave us alone!"

Shocked and frightened, he struggled yet again to break free, but the black flame crawled up his arm suffocating his whole body.

"Forgive me! Forgive me! I am sorry. I did not mean to touch your tail!" He shouted loud enough to wake himself up completely.

Blurred and confused, he woke up to notice the complete halt of bickering between Fuzen and Syric. Koldiar panicked yet again, thoroughly forgetting all about his dream and his unorthodox capture for a moment. He tried desperately to move his arms but come to find out they had been tied with rope leaving only his legs free to dangle. What made it worse was it seemed he was being taken somewhere in the back of a rickety carriage. Apparently, after Koldiar passed out, Orien had decided to lead everyone back to his hideout where they unintentionally packed Koldiar along with their supplies.

Orien had to double take as he drove the carriage when he realized Koldiar was in back.

With a blank face, he calmly asked Syric, "Syric? Why is he back there?"

"You said nothing about not bringing him… Besides, I thought he would be helpful," Syric replied.

"He got knocked out by a pig. How much help is he really going to be?" said Orien.

Hearing that comment, Koldiar was quite insulted. "I am useful too!" said Koldiar.

"See! He thinks so too! And besides, if he is not, we can always use him as bait," Said Syric.

"Yeah! Wait, no, no, no, that is a horrible idea 'cause I am a horrible helping hand and even worse as bait," said Koldiar.

"See! He is deadweight. Even he himself knows it."

Koldiar was just glad that Orien agreed with his agreeance on this matter. Irritated with the whole situation, Syric gave up.

"All right, fine, if you don't want him, then toss him!"

That idea was definitely not an idea Koldiar agreed with and tried to convey his disagreement. Although Syric and Orien had already strongly disagreed to agree with him, Orien abruptly stopped the carriage and picked Koldiar up with Syric's help. Orien counted down while Orien held Koldiar's ropes as Syric held Koldiar's feet.

"On three! One, two, thr—"

But before they could toss him out, Fuzen stopped Orien and Syric with a sort of suspicion.

He expressed his need to question Koldiar. "Kid, do you have faith?"

"Hmm, no?"

"Are you sure? Tell us what you were dreaming just now." Fuzen mentioned to the two to put the kid down.

After Koldiar explained all the weird dreams he had been having, there was an awkward silence, which jwas broken by Orien's deep judgmental voice. "Hmm, strange… Okay, Syric, use your legs this time," shifting his weight to grab Koldiar's ropes.

"Wait!" Fuzen shouted and grabbed Orien's arm. "Even if he does not have faith, he apparently has some connection to this dragon's tail we are trying to find. We could use him to make our job easier."

Orien paused to think, and in a large commanding voice, he said, "Okay, team, obviously this kid has a connection with this 'dream dragon' and our 'money dragon,' so I say we keep him around and see if he could lead us to it."

That blatant display of plagiarism left Fuzen a little more dumbfounded than what he had like to admit. Still, through all this blathering, Koldiar's claustrophobia overwhelmed him, and he lashed out as if he lost his mind.

"I have no idea who any of you are. You abducted me, and now you want me to help? Well, here is something I want—I want to be untied, and I want to exit this carriage like a normal person! And just in case I was not clear, I have no want to go anywhere but back to my treehouse!"

Koldiar's teeth began to sharpen, and his arms began to swell, forcing the rope fibers to strain. As soon as one of the ropes snapped, "A-a-a-r-r-r-g-g-g-h-h-h!" was all you heard after a loud bang, leaving everything to go dark for Koldiar for a third time. Yes, Orien had bashed him in the head with a skillet but mostly out of reflex.

Many hours had passed before Koldiar woke up, but when he did, he was in the woods not far from the road and bound to an old multicolored eucalyptus tree; he was completely by himself in a poorly assembled campsite. He was irritated not because he was imprisoned but because he was just far enough away from the campfire to feel a tease of warmth. Aside from still feeling a bit dazed from his mild concussion, Koldiar spent the rest of his time yelling for help 'till the day became dusk.

Lurking close by, someone did indeed answer his call, but this someone was probably the worst someone to do so. After a while, Koldiar had tuckered himself out, and moments after his last cry for help, he closed his eyes to take a quick nap. At least that was what he told himself, although the reality was, he had given up. Before he nodded off, he was jarred awake by an innocent "Hello!" by what appeared to be an unassuming little boy.

"Hello?" said Koldiar, so confused because as far as he knew, no one was around, not even chirping birds. No one, not one soul was there to watch his anguish, so he ignored the "hello" until he could not because he felt something hitting his leg.

"Mister?" said a little boy lying down at his feet.

A pale, frosty-haired little boy gazed up with a perplexed look about him. His garments would have looked brand-new if they were not slightly ripped and scuffed with dirt.

Koldiar desperately begged the little boy to free him, but it was as if the little boy did not see the harm in letting him stay tied up. On the contrary, he was glad he was able to ask more questions of why he was there in the first place. Koldiar knew he had to calm down, or else he would scare off his only chance of freedom. So he indulged the little boy and asked him his name.

"My name is Koldiar. What is your name, little boy?" he said with a mildly shaky voice.

"Hmm, no one ever asked my name before," the boy replied, and there was an awkward pause before he answered, his eyes widened as he looked to the ground in disbelief. "My name is Nomi...," he answered hesitantly.

After pleasantries, their conversation was rather nice overall. They spoke mostly about all that had led up to their unorthodox meeting. Nomi empathized with Koldiar and agreed that what had happened was deplorable although funny. The boy kept bringing the conversation back to the dragon in Koldiar's dreams, seeming more interested in it than anything else Koldiar had talked about.

"Hey, mister, you know it is not normal to be able to describe a dragon in such detail. My mommy told me dragons are rarely ever seen because they hide in different forms."

"Is that so? How does she know if they are so rare?" "My mommy knew because she met one once!"

It was then Koldiar thought to himself, maybe there is more to these dreams. Maybe I should at least go with those idiots and see for myself. But on his face, he looked as if he did not believe Nomi.

"I am serious! She met her and made friends with her and…and helped her find a place to live!"

"Whoa, whoa, I believe you. I believe you! Could you tell me where the dragon lives?"

"Nope, it is secret," completely mocking him at this point. Koldiar just chuckled to himself and looked at the night sky. "Hey, you know the day is kind of late. You should be at home,
right?"

"He he, you are funny mister. You need not worry about me. I am already home." Nomi snickered as he replied.

That sentence marked the beginning of Koldiar's uncomfortable feelings.

"Hmm, well, okay, could you help me off this tree then? My leg has been asleep for the past three hours, and I should really get going. Those guys will probably be back soon."

At that moment, the sun had set on Koldiar's last chance of escape.

Nomi smiled and ever so sweetly as he replied, "You know what, I was not sure before, but I think I made up my mind… I think I am gonna eat you."

Not hearing him fully, Koldiar said, "Oh, thank you. I really appreciate it. Wait, what?" Koldiar looked at the child with a terrified look.

"I plan to eat you… I will eat every part of you." Just then, Koldiar realized that this innocent-looking child was not a child at all but a mynor. Old tales say that mynors are creatures of chicaneries that lurk on dusty trails or in lonely forests only to trap and eat kind men and women whilst appearing to be lost children.

Hearing Nomi's plans turned Koldiar's feelings into a melting pot of terror, confusion, and an internal high-pitched scream. It burnt a discomfort in his belly as the boy moved closer to him, donning the most unsettling smile. He opened his mouth wider than any surly crocodile showing his razor-sharp teeth and slimy tongue that split into two. The smell that lingered from the gape of his throat was that of gasoline and rotten flesh.

For all of Koldiar's internal screaming, he could not make a sound, so the only thing he could do was close his eyes and hope that the putrid stench burning his nostrils would kill him first. Koldiar's head was completely engulfed to the point where he could feel the boy's needle-tipped teeth starting to puncture his neck.

Just before Koldiar literally lost his head, the overly cautious creature heard crackling sticks in the distance and ran off. Orien, Fuzen, and Syric obliviously walked back from a nearby town with a few sacks of food bickering about money.

"You owe me ten silver for those potatoes and thirty for that duck," said Fuzen.

"What you have to understand is, I would have paid for them, but you did it first," Orien replied.

"You said you did not have any more money!" Fuzen said shrilly. "Well, I knew you were a good friend."

Before Fuzen could reply, Koldiar shouted, "Help me! Get me out of here, please!"

"Give it up, kid. You are not getting out until you finish helping us." Syric scoffed louder than Koldiar's shouting.

"You all are not understanding. There is a little boy here, and he is trying to eat me!"

Yet before anyone could process such a bizarre statement, three large eucalyptus nuts, the size of apples, were hurled from the dense treetops, rendering everyone but Koldiar utterly unconscious. The excited youngster leapt from the trees, gathered his spoils, and tied them all together to the tree. All of them are now stuck to this rough bark that shined more now with the reflection of the moon.

"Surely all of us would be too filling for you, Nomi, and honestly, between you and me, I am a bit spoiled. So maybe y-you could let me go, at least?" said Koldiar.

"Ha ha ha, Koldiar, you know I want to eat you first." The child gleefully laughed.

Koldiar felt stupid for even asking and even more stupid because he noticed everyone was awake, staring daggers at him for trying.

Pleased with himself, a tad tired, and considerably hungry, the child hurried to set up a respectable roasting fire for the first hot meal he has had in a while. The fire was raging along with a nauseous feeling of anxiety in the air. If it were not for the fact that this creature was about to eat them, it was most definitely the fact that he was so excited about it. He had a pouch with assorted seasonings and stated what blend he was going to use for them specifically.

"For Koldiar, I want to taste as much as possible, so I think I will just use salt. For the old one, I will use niffle spice. The fat one gets the hmm…lacfine. Ow, the yikyak would be perfect for the gnome!"

Clearly, he wanted a meal worthwhile, and through all the terror, Syric had an idea.

"No no no! You are going to do it all wrong!" Syric said as the others jeer at his gull to escalate the situation more.

"If I am going to be eaten, I will not let you prepare me the wrong way."

More interested than ever, the child got exceedingly close to Syric to hear his suggestions. "Go on."

Refraining from breathing in Nomi's breath, he blurted out, "Meat Fruit!…yeah, I use it in everything…"

"Hmm…are there any around here?"

Losing breath, Syric struggled to say, "Right up the road on the left."

And without missing a beat, Nomi ran off to pick as many as he could.

When he was gone, the rest of the men complimented Syric's quick thinking and trickery. Though Syric confessed that he was not lying to Nomi, he accidentally told the truth to get him away.

Knowing that, Orien said, "Fool! He will be back any moment!

All right, wizard, time to show your worth, get us out of here." But Syric was not the only one that had a confession.

"I cannot," Fuzen said with disappointment. "What do you mean you cannot!" said Orien.

"I thought you were a professor or something." Syric shrilled.

"I am…but also a little bit cursed… I can do the spells—correction, I could do spells. I just cannot remember them most of the time, and right now is one of those times…"

This was definitely one of those times. Fuzen could not even think of the most basic spell no matter how hard he tried.

"I got nothing," said Fuzen with such shame.

The men were trapped like bat mites having no way to gnaw their way out of imminent demise. At least, that was what they thought when Nomi came back with arms full of meat fruit. It was not long before he had the fire set up and was ready for Koldiar to be roasted alive.

But as Nomi tried to untie him, the fire blazed ten feet tall, and a deep demonic voice commanded, "Let them go! Their bodies and souls belong to me! Leave now or feel my wrath!"

Nomi falls to his knees begging for forgiveness. Apparently, he took no chances with other worldly beings.

"Let me free them and make things right."

"No! Hmm, just go…and no harm will befall upon you," the voice started to sound panicky.

Desperate to make it right, Nomi glanced back to see the sneaky little gnome frantically trying to cut the rope.

The fire extinguished the embers, and it was then pitch-black when Nomi charged on all fours, furiously yelling, "Liars!"

A half a second before Nomi pounced, Fuzen broke free of his restraints, and with one spell in mind, he made the sound oh-fah-ah!

Nomi fell to the ground and limped.

Once Orien was free, he casually grabbed his war hammer that was ever so rudely stripped from him and said, "Okay, men, time to kill it!"

He was heartbroken by the thought of killing something that resembled a child.

Koldiar and Fuzen rushed over to stop him from maiming this childlike creature, but Orien could not tolerate it.

"Look here, wizard, you are already on my list for almost getting me killed, and you, boy, g-get ou—Do you want to go back to sleep!" he angrily yelled, wagging his hammer in Koldiar's face.

"No, of course not, but you want me to help without a struggle! Something tells me I should find this dragon. So just spare him, and I will go with you guys."

"Fine. Just tie him up…a lot." Conflicted, Orien reluctantly agreed.

So it was done. Koldiar tied Nomi up to the same eucalyptus tree, and before they left, Nomi had one last thing to say to Koldiar. "Thank you for not killing me, mister. I knew I made the right choice on trying to eat you first."

Koldiar did not know how to feel about that, but all of them knew that they had quite enough of Nomi for one night. As a result, they eagerly packed up and rode through the night only stopping to relieve themselves.

I am sure most of them would agree that their appetite was completely spoiled for a while.

CHAPTER 5

Whispering Leaves

Early that foggy morning, Koldiar and his gaggle of miscreants traveled around the grand cherry blossom of Wallacgrum following the road to Agisshara—a somber province led by its stocky Botchnoch leader named Pill Beartone. Mr. Beartone is not a king; though he acts otherwise, he is merely a proxy for King Fayos. Even though his decisions were usually seeded in greed and ignorance, he, and the people of Agisshara lived in harmony with its surrounding forest. Whether it be imps, nymphs, fiends, or creeps, Agisshara had built a healthy relationship with all of them. Unfortunately, all that good will end with peepers—dangerous birds that were as bald as they are infuriatingly loud.

There was a bitter taste and a soggy feeling lingering in the air while Orien and Syric slept in the back of the carriage; Koldiar and Fuzen sat in front, steering. It seemed as if nature was trying to warn them of the danger they were riding into.

But it was ultimately ignored when Koldiar said, "Hey, wizard—"

"Fuzen," Fuzen said, correcting Koldiar. "Hmm?"

"My name, it is Fuzen Waycon."

"Oh, sorry. I just figured…never mind. Fuzen, you seem to be the most reasonable person here. Who are these guys?"

"Well, from what I gather, the small one is named Syric. He is some sort of loudmouth thief, I suppose, and the fat one is most undoubtably a conman named Orien."

"And you?"

"Me? I used to be a professor teaching new wizards and holy knights how to really use their magic…but now I am just trying to make some money for my daughter."

"You taught Hayah holy knights! I thought only knights can teach knights."

"Quite the contrary, a hundred years ago, King Gallamar Fayos discovered that being open to learning from the world around you makes for a stronger, a more steadfast Hayah Knight."

"Would it not be harder for you to teach them?"

"Surprisingly no, the only difference between teaching Hayahs and wizards is knowing where their power comes from and how they use it. Hayahs use their faith to cast spells in order to protect using offense as the primary focus and smiting down the wicked as a secondary. Wizards, on the other hand, use their knowledge of nature's energy to manipulate it with sounds. Unfortunately, with all our talents, wizards have no direction. Therefore, most of us end up wandering the world or committing ourselves to the arts."

"Oh, that is why you asked if I had faith."

"Indeed, faith sometimes grants a sort of intuition of one's calling."

"My father never told me about this, and he always wanted me to have faith at all cost. But I never really understood."

"Your father?"

"He was a Hayah Knight for the Eighth Center Court Guard." "Extraordinary, the eighth center? He must have been rather exceptional to be a personal guard. What might his name be? Perhaps I met him?"

"Altiah Neir."

"The Altiah Neir? I never met him, but I have heard many stories, mostly of how he saved the royal family. I am sorry for your loss, but you must be proud. He died a hero! Werewolves are nothing nice, so for him to kill one, he really did deserve the statue they built."

Koldiar instantly felt uncomfortable with where the conversation was headed and had to change it quick.

"Heh…yeah, he does… By the way, why are you not a professor anymore?"

"Hmm…let us just say one tends to lose credibility and often your job when you cannot remember spells."

Apparently, Koldiar touched a slight nerve, making Fuzen continue.

"Even though you give that school the best years of your life, going so far as to help the headmaster grow his leg back, because he could not keep his nose out of the lickweed! Yeah! I still remember that, Garrett!"

Koldiar had no reply for Fuzen's issues, nor did he want to. "Sorry for asking…hmm…not to change the topic entirely, but can I ask how I am supposed to use my faith to help us find this dragon's tail?"

"Hmm…anyway, from the moment you spoke about your dreams, I could feel something that connects you to our dragon, but as for how you can help, I do not know just yet. Though for now, you can just use that insane strength of yours to be our extra muscle until we find out."

That information was not completely satisfying for Koldiar, but it was good enough for the moment.

Later that morning, the bitterness in the air intensified the closer they grew to the forest's boundary—so much so that Syric and Orien awakened, smacking their lips with a detestable look upon their faces.

"What died and crawled into my mouth?" said Syric with the same kind of groggy, confused look as Orien.

Everyone was burdened with the putrid taste that made Nomi's breath seem rather delightful. It was almost unbearable to breathe until they realized they could not actually smell anything. It was all taste that repugnantly insulted their senses. That was a sign; the Stain Forest was getting closer. Over a steep hill, their voyage gifted their eyes with the widest stretching forest in all of Railam. Passing through the threshold of the forest, everyone happily realized they could breathe out their mouth again.

Once inside, there was a sign stating, "Death to those who hear the bird's song." Unfortunately, no one could read the Botchnock it was written in. So it was ignored, forgotten, and never brought up.

With all things considered, most of the ride through the forest was rather peaceful. They even took a short break to set up a cooking pit for lunch.

Koldiar took this time to ask Orien. "Why do you all even want the dragon's tail in the first place?"

Unsure about a good lie, Orien stuttered in a high-pitched voice, "That uh…research, yeah for alchemy!"

"What? I thought it was to keep the king from dying so he can give us as much gold as we can carry!" Syric confusingly blurted out.

Orien leaned over to Syric, muttering under his breath, "Shut up!"

"All of you are trying to save the king? Why not tell me that from the beginning? My dream is to become a Hayah, and just like my father's duty was to protect the king, so should it be mine," Koldiar declared.

Orien's voice became high-pitched once again. "Oh yeah, no, yeah…that is our number one mission—got…to save the king!"

Meanwhile, as they were talking, there were no more than twenty bald pelican-like peepers peeping down at them from on high in the densely packed treetops. Just like a group of lions is called a pride because of their regal nature and a clique of owls is called a parliament because of their wisdom, peepers are called a snatch because of what they did to Koldiar, Orien, Fuzen, and Syric as they lunched. All twenty peepers started to squawk as if they were singing. At first, it was not noticeable, but as time went on, the volume of the squawk got louder. It only took five minutes to seduce everyone; first, it was the two horses to walk off into a trance; third and fourth were for Syric and Orien to walk off silently. Lastly, Koldiar and Fuzen unluckily followed. They all walked single file deeper into the forest, following the sounds of the squawks.

They walked for what had to be hours, and it was not until they were led to the nest of all nests. It was the size of three houses weaved together with sticks, branches, logs, mud, bones, and wood from wagons. Peepers are lazy-packed animals; they all live together hypnotizing larger, more capable animals to build their nest or gather their food. In most cases, hypnotized creatures are forced to be part of the nest if their young are not hatched yet. Otherwise, they are offered to the hatchlings as nourishment for their feeble bodies. However, after the baby peepers mature, they become vegetarians.

Take that information as you will; luckily, as they crumpled over twigs and leaves, they also walked over big shards of eggshells. Koldiar, Orien, Syric, and Fuzen all worked effortlessly to support the nest with branches, mud, logs, and even their horses. They worked five days and six nights and then eventually built themselves into the nests walls as well.

An hour passed, and the sun barely pierced through the lowest reaches of the land. The nest began to rumble, and birds began to squawk, but this time, it was not to order their workers around; it was to sound alarm. If you have ever seen a panicking snatch of peepers, you would know they do not handle surprises very well. They form a ball by flying into one another, trying desperately to protect their queen.

Through the panicking, Koldiar was released from his trance, hearing screams from his men.

"When did I get here?" said Fuzen. "Why is it dark?" said Syric. "Where is my chicken?" said Orien.

"What is happening!? I can barely see!" Koldiar said frantically. Not only could he barely see but also, he could barely move. However, what he could see peering through the thickly packed nest was a ball of swarming peepers being attacked by something large and blue, swooping in and eating them as fast as Koldiar could blink. The last swoop broke through the pack and ate the queen. All the peepers from that moment scattered, flying in fear of this unknown predator and their lack of a leader.

There was a slow, creaking noise before a loud crash toppled over the nest down the side of a steep hill. Barreling down the hillside at unrelenting speed, all that could be heard from a distance were the distorted curling screams from the bowling nest. The nest smashed on a shockingly sturdy oak tree, obliterating any remnants of the peeper's home. A conglomerate of miscellaneous building scrap that riddled the ground as Orien, Fuzen, Syric, and Koldiar arose from crumbled disarray of mud and sticks.

Everyone groaned as they stretched their achingly sore bodies. That was when Koldiar realized there was another man buried within the nest below him.

"Guys there is another man in here. I think he needs help!" Koldiar yelled while trying to dig this poor man out of his mudlike coffin.

"Leave him. He is dead," Orien said, dismissing the situation. "But I just heard him say help," Syric said.

"I said he is dead!" persisted Orien, but just like most things he said, it was blatantly ignored.

Koldiar just continued to dig the trapped man out of the hardened mud and sticks. When this man climbed out, they all noticed he was a

Botchnoch man (they could tell by the way his knees were inverted). He grabbed Koldiar's hands and placed them on his forehead.

"Thank you! Thank you, bless Jehovah! You men are absolutely upstanding. Could any of you tell me where I am?"

"We were hoping you would know."

"Well, luckily, it is daylight still, so it should not be hard to find the way. You would not believe how many times those blasted birds have kidnapped me! But Jehovah always finds a way! Um, would you kind fellas mind escorting me back to my home?" he said ever so graciously.

"Um, yeah, of course. We can help you—" Koldiar replied. "But only for a price," said Orien, cutting Koldiar off.

"We were on our way to town, anyway. You do not have to pay us," Koldiar continued.

"You all saved my life, and as my mother named me Arthur Jerry, of course, I am going to repay you! The only way the Jerry family knows how."

"Finally, someone who is reasonable," Orien said.

"I will serve you all wine and pies for your assistance and a place to stay if you need it," said Arthur.

Fuzen and Koldiar seemed rather happy with this offer, but as for Syric and Orien, they were agitated because it was not something in the gold category.

As Arthur, Koldiar, and Fuzen walked ahead, Orien leaned over to Syric, saying, "Oh, I am getting my gold reward."

CHAPTER 6

After walking through dense, swampy glop for what felt like hours, the wisemen and their new acquaintance reached the land of Agisshara. Whereby no surprise, Arthur successfully led them all to the town of Botchnoch and kept to his word and rewarded everyone for their heroic deeds in his tavern. He treated Koldiar, Orien, Fuzen, and Syric to all sorts of delicious wines and pies; there were red wines, white wines, blue wines, and pink wines all accompanied by its own explicit pie. He served Nicing berry pies with a nice rose and sweet fruit pies with a white wine. The second wave included blue Zoudabaker pies with red wine, but the one they all loved the most was the ginger sugar cream pie with a blue Zinfandel wine. He fed them until their bellies were aching, and their eyes struggled to stay open. As nice as Arthur already was, he even offered them a stay in his tavern's storage room, which they all accepted and thanked him kindly.

That morning, they woke up sluggish from their respective corners of the cramped closet. Their plans were to check around town to find out if there were any dragon sightings. Orien and Fuzen were to check the west side as Koldiar and Syric focused on the east side. However, while they were out asking people about a dragon or about tails, they were either rudely dismissed or an occasional fight would start. Apparently, while they were preoccupied with the peeper situation, King Fayos himself had escorted a copy of the royal decree himself to Agisshara.

"Your Royal Highness, King Christopher Axmil Fayos, calls for every man, woman, and child to set forth a nationwide manhunt for a tail of a dragon. Locations of the said tail are suspected to be within the regions of Agisshara, Salam, or Fahsoom. Within my power, those who succeed will be granted one prize of their choosing."

In short, even if someone knew something, no one had any plans of helping after reading this. So Koldiar, Orien, Fuzen, and Syric decided to regroup back at Arthur's tavern.

Once there, they realized how unpopular Wine and Pies actually was. There were a total of four people inside the building by the time the afternoon fell. Arthur Jerry, the one who ages the wine, and his brother, Gylon Jerry, the one who serves the guests, ran the tavern. One drunkard passed out over his pie at the bar. Then finally, there was a person seated in the far back corner of the room. It was hard to see this person as they were blocked from view by a small pile of pie pans and a few wine bottles. This someone munched and slurped, barely taking time to breathe. It was really quite distracting to those awake in the tavern, especially when no one could actually see her disgusting display of gluttony (as if she even cared). A few pie pans knocked over to reveal the Diggle pixie, Fonfon, finishing her latest bottle of wine and gobbling away at her cobbler, easily eating three times her weight in food.

Koldiar, Fuzen, Orien, and Syric sat and planned to come up with another plan, but no one could pitch an idea for lack of focus. Serious planning turned into jokes and meaningless bets.

"I bet that you could not last a whole day without stealing. You would steal paint off a wall if you thought it was worth anything," said Syric, baiting Orien to take the bet.

"See, I am insulted by your lack of faith in my self-restraint, but I will take that bet. Ten gold sound good?" Orien asked.

"Deal," Syric agreed.

Fuzen jumped in, saying, "Ooh, this should be good! I got twenty on the talking stump!"

They would have continued to go off topic and physically fight if it were not for the disruptive pixie yelling, "Waiteer! I need more pieeee! Right now rather than lateer!" in a sloppy drunk manner.

Seeing something like that was the equivalent of seeing an imp starting a charity. It was extremely unheard of for a pixie to ever eat anything more exotic than flower petals or fruit, let alone to be comfortable in a public place with no contempt about being drunk. These antics would never be condoned by any nymph society.

Arthur quickly went to her beck and call and then proceeded to take the twiglike woman's order. He seemed to be very cautious with his word as she ordered three more pies and another bottle of white wine. She kindly tipped him with a small sparkly diamond that only Syric was able to notice.

Before Arthur could walk back to his lockbox, Syric pulled him to the table, asking, "Arthur, what is the story on the pixie over there?" "I do not know much, but we found her late one night eating leftover pies I threw away. When I confronted her, she tried paying for it with a few sticks and moss. Poor thing panicked when I refused them, but when she offered me her favorite rock, I almost fainted when I saw it was a blue teardrop diamond! Could you believe that, my friend? She has been coming back every other day, bringing more and more diamonds," Arthur replied.

"Yeah, that is pretty remarkable," said Fuzen.

"Unfortunately, the only downfall is, she gets really drunk and will not leave what little guests I have alone, and I have no clue where she gets them from, but who needs to ask when Jehovah is making you a very rich man! As long as she keeps bringing those blue diamonds, she can have the stage if she wants!"

Koldiar started to get lightheaded as Arthur walked away. A short memory flashed before him; it was of the blue dragon from his dreams. Surrounded by a starry night sky, the blue dragon snarled with tremendous fury; all the while, it was crying. The tears that rolled off her face solidified midair, clinking as they hit the ground. They had not turned into glass, but they were blue diamonds. The very same diamonds that the pixie frivolously gave away.

By the time Koldiar came to his senses and was about to go speak to the little pixie, Fuzen, Syric, and Orien had already started talking to her.

"Small-winged, child! Where have you been finding them shiny rocks?" Orien asked, trying to seem friendly but accidentally coming across as a creep.

Completely drunk, Fonfon replied, "There are millions of them, but Fonfon will never tell you!"

Orien poked Fonfon, saying, "Listen here…"

But his intentions fell short when she fell over in hysterical laughter—so much so that she struggled to breathe while clenching her stomach. They all looked at each other confused and mildly irritated by her obnoxious laughing and wheezing.

She begged for it to stop, "Stop! Stop! You win, I give up!" even though no one had touched her.

Syric got extremely irritated and impatient with the drunk pixie, so he ripped a map of Agisshara off the wall and slammed it on the table, knocking down all of Fonfon's pie tins she had collected.

"Where on the map did you find those stones?" Fuzen said to her in a stern fatherlike voice that seemingly scared her. Fonfon hesitantly obliged by pointing at the map.

"I…I found them here…here and here…," she continued, obviously taunting him. "Here, heeere, and here."

By that point, Fuzen could not help but to feel stupid, belittled, and more annoyed than he would like to admit.

"Especially not here, deep inside this cave, inside a ruin. Shush…like I would tell you anything. Fonfon's mind is a steel trap. Pfft, idiots!" Fonfon said, concluding her obnoxious joke.

Fuzen and Orien were the first to realize, and then it took a nudge for Syric to figure out that Fonfon gave up the location on accident. Orien quickly apologized for disturbing her, completely playing along with her ruse.

When they went back to their table, Koldiar told them, "I think those diamonds came from the dragon we are looking for."

"Really? Hmm, well, good because we just found out where the diamonds are," said Fuzen.

"All right, men, we have a 'one stone and two birds' situation.

We leave out in the morning!" Orien declared.

■■

When leaving the following morning, everyone deeply thanked Arthur Jerry for his hospitality and rode off in a horse-drawn wagon, although this would have been a touching farewell if the wagon had not been chased by an extremely angry pie maker screaming in the distance. Why was this otherwise nice man angrily cursing at the top of his lungs? It was because it was Arthur's wagon they stole, unfortunate for Arthur but lucky for them. He was too far away to be heard, especially while Orien nervously hummed loud enough to mask Arthur's colorful Botchnoch language.

"It was really nice of Arthur to help us out with this ride, huh?" Koldiar joyfully asked Orien, who was driving said stolen wagon.

"Hmm? Yeah. Yeah, real nice," he said in his high-pitched lying voice.

Syric leaned over to Orien, asking, "He did not give us the wagon, did he?"

Unable to lie, Orien just handed over ten gold pieces.

CHAPTER 7

Wisemen Say

Riding along the woodsy roads of Agisshara, Syric purposed a very unrelated topic, mostly out of boredom, but Syric had never been good at filtering out random thoughts.

"So since we have formed this unruly band, it would be wise to name our elite group—a name that will bind us together as a fellowship!"

"Well, do you have any purposing thoughts?" asked Orien. "Yes, actually, Syric and his merry men!"

"I was actively ignoring you before, but even I could not let that name be an option."

"Hold on, wizard. How about the name 'the short-horned alliance'!"

"No no no! You are the only one with horns."

"It is not my fault you all aren't perfect."

"Wisemen," muttered Koldiar, grabbing Syric's attention as he continued, "the four Wisemen…"

"Now if you have to have a title—and I do not think we do— that name has my vote."

"Ah, the four Wisemen…I like it!" "As do I! Wisemen it is!"

At that moment of complete irrelevance, the horse pulling the carriage was suddenly spooked by a woman crossing the road dressed in a cobalt cloak that shrouded everything but a lantern with a peculiar blue flame. Syric's first thought was a demon based on the fact she wore a cobalt cloak. Apparently, he read something about how demons use flashy blue cloaks to drag you to hell.

Although there was some truth to his knowledge, legend stated that if a blood moon was present during a lunar Marti Gras, a demon could sneak out of hell by wearing a cloak. Despite the fact that it was insanely rude to accuse or assume someone was an actual demon, the lunar Marti Gras was eight months away, and it was broad daylight. On top of all that, he wanted to fight the woman he thought was a demon.

While Syric was rightfully being held back by Fuzen (who actually knew the legend), Orien caught a glimpse of a black tail heavily curtained by the dance of the blue-flamed lantern.

"Maiden! Maiden! A moment of your time, please."

Without looking his way or even turning, the woman in cobalt stopped to hear his words.

"By order of King Fayos of Wallacgrum, the four Wisemen are contracted to procure and deliver the dragon's tail in your possession!" Orien said, holding the map, pretending that it was an official document.

However, when Orien looked back at her, she had already darted through the woods to their left.

"Come on, she has the tail!" Orien shouted as they all leaped out of the carriage to pursue on foot. After chasing her for a while, it was clear she was toying with them until all they could chase was a distant chuckle. As they were standing back-to-back and not knowing what direction the now menacing laugh was coming from when suddenly, a wall of flames circled them.

"Wizard!" Orien said.

"I got nothing," Fuzen said shrilly.

"Of course not," Orien replied just as they heard the woman's echoing voice say, "The tail you all foolishly seek does not belong to you nor your king! This was the first and only time you all shall see the tail. If you value your lives, then heed my warning—leave us alone!" A powerful gust of wind then blew the flames that surrounded them cold.

Moments later, a loud crunching crash could be heard near the carriage. Somehow, that woman not only managed to corner the Wisemen but also managed to thoroughly destroy their carriage before she left.

Though Koldiar was discouraged from going any further, everyone else was supernaturally motivated by the progress of seeing their objective up close. Orien, Syric, and Fuzen nonchalantly packed whatever was left of their belongings that had not been crushed, burned, or squished and continued down the road as if their lives had not been threatened.

"What are you doing?" Koldiar asked.

"We are going to get the tail?" Orien replied, highly confused by Koldiar's question.

"We were almost killed by some magical woman that has what we are after!" yelled Koldiar.

"Look, as a boy, great Ahma always told me, 'Boi, always get da gettings while da gettings ar' good. Even if da gettie knows your ar' trying to get their gettings, just befuddle da gettie to make da gettings good again.' Get it?"

"Not even a little bit," Koldiar replied.

"His thieving grandmother taught him to steal whenever he saw a chance and swindle people when he did not," Fuzen clarified.

"Don't you talk about great Ahma like that! She was a decent Jehovah-fearing woman, bless her soul."

"She literally taught you how to be a charlatan!" Fuzen said. "Orien, I know your great Ahma. Last year, she sold me a horse that I paid her to take care of. Until a month ago, I found out it has been dead for eight years."

"He he he, the old dead horse's trick. Anyway, the point is, we know it is real, and we know where to find it. All we need to do is distract her and the dragon."

"Hmm, for some reason, I do not feel good about this quest," Koldiar said.

"Do you want to do the Hayah thing and save King Fayos or not? Who knows he may make you a real Hayah," Orien slyly persuaded.

"Fine, I will keep going for King Fayos and to honor my father!" he declared.

"Uh, good, good for you," Orien muttered.

Upward and onward, the Wisemen followed the road until the next morning where they were greeted by a surprisingly pleasant morning. Halfway to the destination, marked by Fonfon, Koldiar had a feeling they were being watched. He twisted his neck until it was sore, desperately trying to watch his own back. Then from the corner of his eye, he saw a Nubian woman within the trees, glowing in her white gown. However, when he tried to look at her straight on, her glow fully blinded him, if not but for a moment.

When his sight came back, Koldiar's curiosity drew him to look again, but the mysterious woman was missing, but he could feel she was not gone. Trying to convince himself that it was nothing but his imagination, Koldiar suddenly stumbled across a white book glowing just like the woman he saw.

Koldiar's name was boldly embroidered in the face, and the first page wrote, "He who is named by this book is read by this book. Its answers are that of future questions."

"So…this book will read me and answer a question I have not asked yet? Fuzen, do you know anything about this?" Koldiar asked. "I have never learned of any such items that read the reader,"

said Fuzen.

"Should I turn the page?" Koldiar asked, even though he planned to anyway.

"The responsible part of me says no, but the wizard in me says this item is too rare to pass up! So open it!" Fuzen said.

No one objected to his curiosity in lieu of their own equally intense curiosity. When Koldiar flipped to the second page, it was blank—that is, until words appeared before their very eyes as if someone was there writing his story.

The text wrote, "For the man halved with another must find his faith by saving his lover."

"Oh, a lover. Who is the lucky lady? Hmm?" Syric probed.

"A lover? No, this cannot be for me. I have been watching the forest alone for the last ten years, and the only woman I know is far from a lover!"

"What does it mean by 'halved with another'?" Fuzen probed. "I-I have no idea," Koldiar said irritably.

"Can I have it?" Orien probed.

"Yeah, keep it. This is all too confusing. Can we just keep going?" Koldiar asked.

"How come he gets to keep it? I am the wizard!" Fuzen asked shrilly.

"You can have it for your pie rations," Orien bargained.

"No! This is not happening again with you!" Fuzen said, now

seeming to stand up to the hefty swindler.

However, after seeing him slowly place the book in his bag, Fuzen gave in.

"Ugh, fine," he said, handing over his last honey apple chicken pot pie.

Koldiar walked side by side with the perturbed wizard and the gleeful charlatan eating his pie. He could not shake the feeling that he may have just seen an angel. Thereafter, Koldiar slowly forgot the book and its confusing words when Orien made him a little hungry for pie too.

CHAPTER 8

A Giga-Disaster

After wandering the forest for a few days trying to find the area Fonfon had pointed out—due to Orien's side sweat bleeding the ink off the map—they were lost. Immensely on edge and highly doubtful, Koldiar, Orien, Fuzen, and little Syric felt no closer to the tail then when they started. Either way, they kept looking effortlessly until they stumbled across a band of scary-looking men led by none other than Victor Stow. From the bushes, they saw him and his henchmen violently thrashing their way through the forest.

This time, he was not in royal armor nor were the men surrounding him. They were dressed in dirt-stained bandage wraps that held their tattered tunics and trousers close to their bodies; in other words, clothing fit only for scoundrels. They were without a doubt Victor Stow's bandit crew.

Koldiar looked to everyone and whispered, "Is that the same man who chased us before?"

"Okay, I have a plan! You and the wizard go over there and cause a distraction to lure them to you. Syric, you go over to the other side and make a goose sound and throw them off. By that time, I will be far away enough," Orien said, trying to take charge of the situation.

"We are not doing any of that," Fuzen replied.

"Then what do you expect us to do?" Orien loudly whispered.

Fuzen tried to think of a plan, but he could not think clearly. He continued, "Well, whatever we do, we need to work together!"

At the same moment that Fuzen said, "Work together," Syric decided it was going to be his time to shine. Trying to knock out a bandit that walked a little too close to their bush, Syric grabbed a rock, cocked his arm back, and flung it with extreme intent. He wanted to do as much damage as possible. The force from that rock would have rendered that man more than just incapacitated if Syric was as accurate as he was strong.

Not only were the bandits utterly confused and on high alert now, but Koldiar, Orien, and Fuzen were all dumbfounded as to why he would ever do such a thing at such an inconvenient time. They all simultaneously asked why in a semi not-so-quiet manner.

All he could say in his defense was, "I thought I could get him." Not a moment had passed before they heard the gleeful voice of Victor Stow chanting behind them, "Well, well, well, if it is not the

fat fool himself! I am going to—"

"Hey! Hey, Victor! How was your nap? Did you have a nice dream about how dumb you are!" Orien replied, interrupting Victor. "I have no time for your childish taunts, and I am tired of your constant backstabbing! You cost me a good position in the castle! Now I am out here looking for a stupid tail to make amends. But you know what? I was hoping I would see you out here so I can watch your eyes roll back as I strangle you to death!"

All the bandits started to surround them, making their presence known they were there and that they were a threat. Koldiar stood in front of Orien trying to protect him.

"We have gone through too much to let you just kill us now! So if you are going to kill us, then prepare for a fight!" Koldiar said. "Look here, boy, I have no desire for you nor do I want the rest

of your miscreants. All I want is his blood on my blade. The rest of you may leave," Victor said, drawing his sword.

In a nonverbal conversation, Fuzen shrugged his shoulders at Koldiar, silently asking him to consider Victor's generous offer. Koldiar genuinely thought about it and nodded when he realized Orien most likely put himself in this situation, and not to mention he was the one who knocked Koldiar out with a frying pan. For those reasons, Koldiar was fairly confident when he mouthed "Come on" to Fuzen.

"Hey! I am no miscreant!" Syric shouted, completely ruining Fuzen and Koldiar's plan to sneak away.

"Hmm? Oh, my apologies, what I meant was rodent," Victor so smugly said.

Silence fell upon them like a sudden eclipse. The bandits did not know the gravity of the situation, but Orien, Koldiar, and Fuzen did as they watched the words fly out of Victor Stow's mouth as if they were visible, landing in Syric's ears. When they saw Syric's face that had not comprehended what had been said yet, there was nothing. However, when Syric realized what was said, everyone could literally see him morph into a complete rage.

Without even thinking, Syric threw two daggers from his belt, hitting and killing two of the bandits. He charged toward Victor with pure anger, screaming, "Miscreants!" and dodging the two slashing bandits in front of him. By this time, a peaceful outcome expired faster than the guy Syric stabbed in the heart. Orien, Fuzen, and Koldiar swiftly began defending themselves from the horde of bandits that charged in. Orien bashed them left and right with his war hammer. Fuzen stumbled and wobbled, barely dodging the thrust of their swords, and trying to slap them with his staff when he could, all the while trying to remember a spell that would end the whole debacle. Koldiar stole a sword off a dead body, surprising himself by how skilled he still was at practical fighting. He continued to slash, lunge, dodge, and parry like a professional knight. It was definitely all the training he retained from his father shining through.

All the fighting ended abruptly when Syric finally made his way through to Victor. The halfling, with blood in his eye, pounced like a panther straight for his face. Climbing around his body, only stopping to punch him where he could, he then put him in the world's tiniest choke hold. Victor never was any good with pain, so a simple choke hold was more than enough to make this coward man surrender.

However, that victory was short-lived when out of the thickets, a thirty-foot-tall giga-troll awakened from his fall hibernation and threw a tree in the middle of the clearing they fought in, killing the henchman fighting Fuzen. It had heard all the commotion and rushed over to destroy whatever and whomever made the noise. Giga-trolls are random creatures; they never roam in clans due to their fondness of seclusion. The only thing they like most in the world is a nice deep sleep. So when their sleep is interrupted, they are prone to blind rage.

"Noise! Stop noise! Light? No! Stop light! Stop noise too!" said the troll while ripping a tree out of the ground and mashing three bandits in front of Syric and Victor.

Koldiar and Fuzen barely had time to jump out of the way. "Syric, I think it is time to go!" cried Koldiar.

Syric let Victor out of his choke hold and hopped over the tree the troll had thrown. It could not have been any worse for Victor's group when the troll picked the tree up again and swung it at the bandit to his left, killing the rest of Victor's henchmen. Koldiar, Fuzen, Orien, and Syric were not taking any chances with fighting any troll or even looking at it. They ran like headless jipdogs through the trees. Outside of sleep, they did not realize giga-trolls love nothing more than to chase their prey. So naturally, running was the worst thing they could have done because that troll got excited and sprinted after them. Of course, the troll could have caught them easily, but like I said, he was having too much fun. As for the escapees, they were scared out of their minds and running for their lives when a

The mountainside blocked them from running any further. "Wizard! Do something!" yelled Orien.

"I am trying!" he lifted his staff in the air the same time the troll sprinted toward them.

"Uh…aye yee fum."

Those sounds he shouted conjured a ball of distorted light that tore through the fabric of time and outer life. Orien and Syric got sucked in first, but before Fuzen was pulled in, he saw Koldiar being snatched away by the giga-troll.

CHAPTER 9

Here and There

On the foreside of the mountain from where Koldiar, Orien, Fuzen, Syric, and the playful giga-troll were, a luminescent white sphere the size of a severed ogre head appeared.

Pulsing rapidly, the sphere regurgitated Orien and Syric out like two pieces of spoiled meat only moments before Fuzen appeared, still trying to grasp at Koldiar.

"Koldiar!" Fuzen yelled, frantically trying to figure out what to do. He grabbed Orien by the collar, forcing him to his feet. "It got him! We have to go back!"

"What do you mea—No! No! If big green and dopey got him, he is already dead!" Orien replied.

"But…he is just a kid," Fuzen said woefully.

"I swear on my mother, wizard, if you get me killed over your emotions, I will haunt you!"

"There is no way he could have survived against that thing," Syric said when something in the sky caught his eye.

He saw him, he saw Koldiar flying like a flailing ragdoll through the sky.

"Hah! There he is! The troll threw him!" Syric obnoxiously shouted before letting out a loud unnecessary cackle.

Fuzen and Orien saw Koldiar falling and ran to try and catch him, but the troll threw him too far for them to help. They knew for certain

Koldiar was going to fall flat and, for lack of a better word, splat. However, as they braced themselves for the gruesome "splat," Koldiar disappeared from plain view. Feeling sort of cheated and a tad confused, they were compelled to search further, and to their surprise, they saw Koldiar had fallen into a canyon. They were just in time to see the unfortunate hermit hit the bottom of the lake with ungodly force.

They were all silent for a moment until Fuzen said, "Okay, now he is dead."

"What do we do now?" said Syric.

"Hmm, we must keep going…find the tail…and become super rich… That is what he would have wanted," Orien said, placing his hand over his heart while Fuzen looked at him in disbelief.

"Are you serious? The boy just died!"

"He would have wanted us to keep going." "He would have wanted to live!"

"Maybe if your magic worked a little better, we would not be in this position, so are you going to come with us or what?"

"Well, yeah, I want my cut. I just wanted it to be a little hard to move on."

"Good. We should get going. The sun is already getting too low. You ready, Syric?" Orien said as he got up from the edge of the canyon.

"Ready!"

When they turned around, they were stunned to see an angry giga-troll thrashing straight for them.

"R-a-a-a-h-h-h-h!" is what the troll said, which I am pretty sure was troll for "Come back and play."

Ignorantly, Fuzen left his spell open for the troll to stumble through.

Looking at his eminent demise charging at him, Orien looked at Fuzen irritably and said, "I hate you, wizard."

But before the troll could grab them, Fuzen grabbed Orien and Syric first, saying, "Well then, you are going to hate me more now." They then jumped into the canyon.

At the same time, the troll dimwittedly fell in after them, plummeting under the large troll, flipping and twisting, barely avoiding being caught by his big green hairy hands.

Through all this disaster, it was quite funny to think of the perspective that the nearby birds must have had, especially when they heard Orien yelling at Fuzen, "You are fired!"

If you would have seen the smile on this troll's face when he eventually caught them—a smile so repulsive even his mother would have gagged. The falling they endured did not last forever nor did the "successful" capture of the remaining Wisemen, although for them it might have. But when it did end, it was over. The troll had fallen backside down, and when the troll's skin touched the water, the pain forced him to relinquish Fuzen, Orien, and Syric. Then gravity forced them to bounce off his bulging belly and into a tunnel in the side of the canyon.

When they landed in the tunnel, the seismic splash made by the troll flushed them down and through the winding tunnel. At the end of the tunnel, they were shot out into an underground forest of "gray lives"—hundreds of glowing trees of white leaves and grey bark with even brighter roots that weaved in and out of the ground, providing light for the whole cave.

"Whoa, is this what that pixie talked about?" Syric said, gathering himself from the soft soil he fell on.

They all were amazed and still a bit shaken up, especially when an unsuspecting howl bounced around the cave walls, sending chills down all their spines.

"I feel something, a dark dwelling here," Fuzen said after placing his hand on a tree.

Out of his damp cloak pocket was a magical writing tool known as Mai Chojk. He used this to write a multicurricular seal on the tree. Then he drew the same symbol on everyone's arm.

"Syric, I need you to put your hand on this seal and repeat after me."

"Why?" Syric said reluctantly to be difficult for the sake of being difficult.

"Because you are the only other person with magical—"

Cutting him off in midsentence was a loud echoing dragon roar.

When it stopped, Fuzen immediately continued, "Talent. Now do you want to cooperate?"

Syric and Fuzen finally had an accord, and Syric followed his orders to a T. He placed his hand firmly on the tree and prepared for something magnificent to happen after repeating after Fuzen.

"Excitant!" Syric said with great gusto, but all that happened was a slight glow from the mark on their arm.

"Is that it? What did I do? Why am I tired?"

"Congratulations, you just performed real magic. As for what we did, we sealed all magic within this cave with the help of the natural magic within the trees."

"Which means…?"

"Which means as long as any of these trees are not damaged, magic cannot be used. So that means—"

"So that means you are still useless. Got it!" Orien said, obviously mocking him.

And as anyone would, Fuzen felt offended, glaring daggers at him. "I am most definitely not useless!"

"So you cannot take a joke or use magic. All right then, lead us to our dragon, wizard."

From there, Fuzen led them the best he could through the thickly bunched trees, cautiously walking to where the roar originated. Another roar startled them.

It has been a while since they all had eaten anything, and they were running out of energy rapidly. Good for them, though they had smelled a smelly smell, but this smelliest of smells smelled good.

"Oh…oh! I smell onions! A-And pork sausage with potatoes!" As soon as Syric said that, all they could think about was smothered sausage and potatoes. They hobbled through the forest, holding their stomachs, completely distracted from their main objective. Oh, how they followed that smell until they approached three large bowls with heaping helpings of meat, potatoes, and peeking bits of caramelized onions. It was as if the heavens were treating them like kings, but as their luck regularly went, it was ultimately the earth treating them like fools. As they shoved gluttonous amounts of food in their mouths, each handful looked less and less like food and more like dirt and bugs.

Needless to say, they spat out what they had not already swallowed and scraped off the dirt that was caked onto their tongues. When they came back to sanity, they glanced up and noticed they were facing a ruin of sorts. It was not a very big building, and most of it was wrecked beyond repair; the rubble had roots weaving through the cracked and shattered cinder blocks. Before them was a thick wooden door, slightly opened and greatly intimidating. A sapphire light flickered between the crack, and all three of them felt compelled to pull the door wide.

Through the door was a circular room filled with eerie wonder; the stone floor was filthy with diamonds with a single lantern in the middle, although the raggedy lantern they saw sitting upon a white pedestal was more intriguing. A strong blue flame lived inside it, burning out intensely the tiny access of the lantern's housing. Its blaze reached over the handle, but the longer they stared at it, the more the flame split apart. Fuzen focused his blinded eyes at its center, revealing to him a stubby clip of a black tail.

"Look at all these diamonds!" said Syric while he and Orien stuffed as many as they could into their satchels, even going as far as to emptying out Fuzen's bag full of his studying papers.

But he did not care because his eyes were glued to the revealed tail.

"This…this is the…tail," said the enticed Fuzen. "How do you know?" said Syric.

"I feel…I feel its power! Also, it is the only thing here that looks like a tail, moron," Fuzen insulted while slowly reaching for it, just to be denied by Orien slapping the glass cage shut and twisting the shudder closed.

"Good job, wizard! Now help with these diamonds before we leave."

"But—" Fuzen said.

"You, okay? You are being a little weird over there," said Orien. "N-No, I am fine," he said.

"Yeah, thought you were going to do something stupid like stick your hand in the fire," Orien said, fastening the lantern to his side and hiding it under his split-hemmed tunic.

As soon as they were about to leave, a tiny voice said, "Who are you?"

Those sudden words straddled them to their core, and they thought it was Nomi again.

Orien took the lead by saying, "We are friends."

"You are not my friend. I do not know you. Echo is my friend, and she would not like you all here. Unless…you guys are her friends too," the voice said.

"Echo? Uh…oh, Echo! Yeah, we know Echo!" Orien said. "You do? Well, in that case, it is nice to meet you all. My name

is Fon Fauna Fon or Fonfon for short!" she said while secretly going back to scavenge for more diamonds. "Are you all dragons too?"

"Yes," said Orien.

"That is fantastic! Let me go tell her you all are here!" Fonfon said.

"No!" they said simultaneously. "Uh, heh, no, she already knows we are here. She told us to clean up," said Orien.

"Oh, okay…well, where is Echo's lantern?" she asked.

"Um, she, uh, took it. Yeah, she took it with her! Shush, you know how she is with that thing."

"Yeah, you are right! It scares me to think that if it went missing, she would destroy everything in her path to get it back. She would not even go easy on me, and I am her best friend. She even gets mad when I look at it too hard. Could you believe that? Ha ha, like I need to tell you all this. You probably already know she would tear anyone into several different itty-bitty pieces."

"Itty…bitty pieces…?" Syric stuttered. "Yep, the smallest, oh, and their families." "Our…families?" Fuzen whispered.

"Yeah, and then take your most loved possession for good measure."

"Oh no, not my money," Orien said shrilly. "But I doubt it would ever come to that."

They were all petrified at the very thought of what Fonfon said. "That is, um, oddly specific," said Fuzen.

"Yeah, she says it quite often actually. Hah, she even threatens me for even being in here when she gets really heated."

"Well, we finished cleaning. It was very nice to meet you. But we must be leaving now," Fuzen said, pulling Syric and Orien together, rushing them to leave.

But as they were leaving, their stomachs collectively rumbled loud enough for Fonfon to notice and giggle.

"Would you all like some food before you leave?"

Despite their best judgment, they accepted. They followed her to a diminutive village where her pixie brothers and sisters resided. As luck would have it, the pixies were just about done cooking.

As they walked up, an elder woman stopped them and demanded, "Fonfon! Where have you been? You were supposed to help gather water for the stew!" The woman continued without taking a breath. "You know we pixies cannot carry much. Lizzy almost drowned trying to hold extra water in her mouth…blessed little thing." The woman paused long enough to insist, "I keep telling the counsel she should be put on special pixie duty, you know, guarding the empty grain pouches." As she came to herself, the woman questioned, "Who are they? They look like humans?" She then said in a loud whisper, "Fonfon, you know better than to bring humans here!"

The moment she said "Humans," the whole workforce of pixies stopped and stared.

Unfazed, Fonfon replied, "Hi, Lady Glady, these are not humans. These are Echo's dragon friends. Um, what are your guys names again?" Fonfon questioned.

"Um, Orien, Syric, and Fuzen," they said in conjunction. "Hmm, and you said these young men are dragons?"

Lady Glady said as she peered deeply into Fuzen's eyes, pinching Orien's fat with her small hands and then sniffing Syric's hair. She then sifted her eyes from the young men to the food and yelled, "Well, good enough for me! We are starving. You all come eat!"

When it comes to pixies, they love to eat together in their village center. They all sat in a circle outside with torches helping illuminate their meal. Fuzen, Orien, and Syric all looked uncomfortable and out of place because of their size. Well, not so much for Syric, but he still felt unusual. Speaking of unusual, the designated hosts of the night placed a pile of grass blades in front of them as another pixie plopped a thick glob of lumpy brown "stew" on top of the pile. This stew was garnished with red rose petals and green nuts, and when everyone was being served, Lady Glady leaned over to Orien, saying, "This is my grandson's recipe. I am so happy to have two grandsons that can cook."

Orien chose not to reply with words—no, his glance at her spoke for him, saying, "Either you are crazy or you think I am because this looks disgusting."

The guys would have eaten absolutely anything else if they had a choice, but seeing there were multiple little eyes around them waiting for a reaction, they were obliged (forced) to try it; to their surprise, the "stew" was not too bad. They thought it was a bit texturally unpleasing, but otherwise, the taste was not half bad. They liked it, but they disliked liking it.

CHAPTER 10

*I feel like I have some sort of destiny. I wonder who this "lover" of mine is…
Everything in my body says that she will be one and the same.*
—Koldiar

Many things were wrong with this moment for Koldiar; no person should ever be treated as a plaything, flung around, shaken up like a baby's rattle by a thirty-foot-tall child. The troll played with him as he tried to struggle. Koldiar had a strong enough stomach not to throw up even though he wanted nothing more than to do so. Maybe it was the boorish shaking or the tense grip of the giga-troll, but whatever the case was, Koldiar was fed up. His teeth sharpened yet again and, ironically, bit the hand that held him. Gouging a plug of flesh and skin out of the troll's index finger definitely got his attention. The giga-troll spiraled out of control, and with his burly arm, the troll pitched Koldiar completely over the mountainside.

Soaring through the air over the small mountain, Koldiar looked like a flailing fish that slipped out of a butcher's hand. All the birds in his way were just as unhappy with his precarious situation as he was. He flew over Orien, Fuzen, and the cackling Syric just before plunging down into a lake-filled canyon.

Slap! was the sound where Koldiar and the water met in disagreement. The wind was forced out of Koldiar's lungs, making him pass out and sink to the bottom of the lake. Teaming schools of pinkish yellow babblefish and bloodred Sullymots curiously swam around him. Naturally, all lakes are still bodies of water, but this lake at the bottom of a canyon leisurely swirled—that is, until he reached the center of the lake where the water rapidly began to whirl. Koldiar's unconscious body had no choice but to listen to the demands of the current and drift deeper inside the unknown hole.

He who believeth in me shall fulfill their destiny…

Koldiar fell from a subtle cascading waterfall and washed up on the edge of a stream. It seemed as though he had warped to another world— the same underground forest illuminated by millions of bright vines, the one Orien, Fuzen, and Syric landed in. Koldiar's abrupt stop and mild drowning jolted him awake. After trying and failing to catch his bearings, he realized he was utterly lost for the first time in his life.

"Oh no, this is not good."

No, this is not good at all! Koldiar thought to himself just before seeing a light bright enough to be daylight. He pulled himself together and hobbled toward it, picking up a long stick to help him walk.

The trees covered in white leaves and gray bark called gray lives do more than provide light for the whole cave with their roots. Old folk knew them as Alberi Subdola because through them, they would reveal the most painfully vivid dreams or a nightmarish past. Koldiar would soon find out why these trees should not be taken lightly. Following a large path that looked to have been trampled through, he saw a young King Fayos on one knee, consoling an even younger version of himself.

"Listen, son, your father was a great man and one of my closest friends, and as much as I would like to believe he sacrificed himself for this kingdom, I know he did it for you. I know he was your only family, and for that, you are welcome to be a part of ours, if you wish."

Little Koldiar wiped his tears and soundly accepted the king's offer. As that dream faded away, Koldiar kept walking through the deformed path to see King Fayos yet again, but this time, he was with his advisor, Marren Pace.

"Sir! Sir, you cannot let that boy remain in this kingdom, let alone this castle!"

"Marren, calm yourself. Nothing happened today because of that boy! He is my son now and will not be banished from his home." "You are right. Today, nothing happened because of that boy,

but because of what he is, people will die because of what that boy is tomorrow! And your precious 'son' will be the death of your kingdom or, worse, your daughter."

"Marren! Leave…leave me to my thoughts. I will decide what to do with him later."

The two royal figures disappeared within the trees, leaving Koldiar alone in his hollow thoughts. Why am I seeing these things? Am I going crazy? Koldiar thought as he wiped his eyes with his right sleeve. He continued to think, perhaps I am asleep. That thought was quickly contradicted after slapping his face repeatedly.

Just when he thought all the visions were over, he heard, "There, there, son, get up and try again. Just plant your feet this time."

"Papa, it is impossible! I feel myself about to trip every time.

Can we just move on?"

Koldiar then saw his younger self and his father, Altur, training within the trees.

"Listen, if you only concern yourself with what is possible, you will never accomplish the impossible! Just believe in yourself and have faith in Jehovah. Now do it again. On guard!"

"Now parry one, Koldiar!" "Follow up with three!"

"Now repost!" drilled Altur, but despite being highly simple moves, they still proved to be too difficult in the woodsy terrain.

"You must control your footwork, son. Power comes from your legs, moving through your body and out the blade of your sword. With no control, there is no power, and with no faith, no divinity," Altur instructed when all of a sudden, the older Koldiar felt a gut-wrenching discomfort and slowly turned around to see a patchy anthropomorphic wolf staring him straight in the face.

Foam fizzled from the corners of its mouth as the look of assimilation distorted its face. Fear quickly lifted Koldiar's feet in the opposite direction, only to be tripped by a looped root. However, the werewolf was an illusion that just ran through him and straight for the illusion of child Koldiar who managed to get his foot tripped in a root. Without thinking and without powers, Altur instinctively jumped in front of little Koldiar, guarding him with his body. Both young and old Koldiar watched helplessly as the werewolf mauled their father to death.

Between each battered attack, Koldiar heard Altur's harrowing screams and then the last words he would ever hear from his father, "Koldiar, run!"

Just after the werewolf's vicious jaw finished him off, little Koldiar tried to flee as his father instructed, but the werewolf was too fast; it lunged toward him, sinking its teeth into little Koldiar's left shoulder.

These illusions of his father dying in front of him and seeing himself being bitten again triggered an excruciating burning in his shoulder. The agony was too much for Koldiar to handle; all of his searing bite marks practically drove him insane. The unbearable searing of his skin forced him to tear his tunic off, revealing his deformed shoulder riddled in scars.

"Aaarrrggghhh!" cried Koldiar.

It was as if the traumatic event happened all over again. The pain eventually subsided, but when it did, he was far too drained from what had happened, so he desperately inched over to a little nook under a bunch of dead roots and then drifted to sleep.

Balled up in his dark corner, he began to change like a feral butterfly; he emerged from the roots with a howl, "Ahhwooooo!"

From that moment further, everything was a blur for Koldiar; he had no control of himself. He trampled through the trees, sniffing out anything he could kill until his nose found someone small, winged, and oddly sweet-smelling. Huffing and puffing, he threw himself forward with all his might. Fonfon was the target of his devilish pursuit.

If it were not for pixie's overly paranoid nature, he would have gotten her, but she noticed him only seconds before he pounced, flying as fast as she could and weaving through branches and trees until she flew out into an open clearing where the mother gray lives stood alone.

Fonfon tried to quickly fly behind a monumental tree as she yelled, "Echo! Help!"

Wolfman Koldiar caught up to her, swatting her out the air and at the feet of a great blue crystal dragon. Their gaze met; Koldiar's bloodthirsty eyes locked with hers until she glanced down at Fonfon laying sprawled before her. Echo's foot moved like lightning stomping the ground in front of Fonfon ready to attack. At that moment, a bellowing blue flame disgorged from the heart of her throat, warding

Koldiar back from trying to charge at her.

"Leave us alone!" she yelled, following with an echoing roar enveloping her words.

Thud-thud, went Koldiar's heart, shocking the sense into him.

He remembered her from his dream.

"You...," he said as his body became his own again and only after painfully morphing back from his animalistic alter ego.

This dragon named Echo should have completely destroyed Koldiar, but she left him alone (though the thought did cross her mind). She was much more concerned with Fonfon's wellbeing and instead shifted her state of being to that of a human woman, which allowed her to better care for her hurt pixie.

Her body sparkled more than any star Koldiar had ever seen. Her scales dazzled until her dragon form disintegrated as if it was made of sand. Kneeling over her friend was a beautiful curvaceous woman wearing a cloak of cobalt somehow made of crystals, which shrouded the purest brown, honey colored skin Koldiar had ever seen. Her face was defined and fierce yet young and supple. Her eyes were jeweled with sapphires that could cut through the hardest diamond. Where there were horns, two hair braids black as onyx took their place, pointing down her back. As for her lips, they were a soft dusty rose in full bloom. The way she carried herself was almost accidentally poised, very precise, and naturally in tune with her body. He found her captivating, absolutely captivating.

"Fon, are you okay?" she said, supporting her head.

"No, I-I am going to die," she replied before trying to move and making a big deal about her scraped leg and slightly bent wing.

She groaned when Echo picked her up; she groaned with every step Echo took, and she groaned because she groaned the wrong way. At this point, you must have noticed pixies do not do very well with pain. Anything more than a slight headache, and these creatures are impossible to deal with (despite being a warrior race). Koldiar could not help but hear all her obnoxious bellyaching, but none of it seemed to bother Echo's patient ears. In fact, she cared for her almost like a seasoned mother.

She coldly brushed past Koldiar, making him feel worse because even though he could not control himself, he saw everything that had happened. He wanted to do something to make it right, but when she passed him, the intoxicating scent of lavender seemed to make him feel even worse; he had to do something. He scrambled through his pockets to find anything to help.

"Perfect!" he said to himself after finding a little jar of his "hunting ointment" or, more accurately, a paste made of garlic, mud, and hog spit he calls ointment. He then proceeded in following her like a lost puppy all the way to a small stream. There she planned to wash Fonfon's "wounds," so now Koldiar had to form a plan to approach her, but not knowing quite how to approach her, he stayed as far back as possible. He realized he had to say something, anything!

Just do it! he thought to himself, and before it was too late, he said, "I have something…that might help," cupping his dusty jar of ointment.

"Hmm, you are still here? What part of leave us alone did you not understand? Or do I need to eat you?" Echo said, kneeling at the stream, not even turning back to look at him.

"N-No! I have had enough of that lately. I just want to help, to show that I am sorry," he said.

"Last time, boy. Leave now," she repeated.

"Okay, I will leave… But if you want the ointment, it is right here," he said after placing his jar on a boulder next to her.

"I am sorry. I will find my way out…somehow."

"Wait," she said, "show me how to apply the ointment, and then I will show you out."

Koldiar's ears perked up, and a bit of a smile stained his face when he rushed to help her.

"A little here and a little there, and that should be all she needs." "What is this stuff? It stinks! Ugh!" Fonfon said shrilly before jumping off the large leaf she was lying on and then flying off in utter disgust.

"Well, it seems your medicine worked," Echo said with a small smirk on her face. She continued, "But now it is time for you to leave. Do not worry, I can carry you out. It will be faster that way."

But after something funny happened, not funny "ha ha" but funny weird, she tried to gather as much soul mana to change back into a dragon, but nothing happened. She tried relentlessly to change, but nothing was the conclusion she came to.

"Maybe we could possibly walk until you regain your strength," Koldiar timidly suggested.

"Very well," she said reluctantly, "stay close to me. This place can be dangerous for you!"

Before walking through the forest, Echo snatched two leaves off a loafed branch.

Handing Koldiar a leaf, he confusingly accepted, saying, "What is this for?"

"Eat it. The trees will think you are one of them and will not play tricks on you," she said as she scarfed down the white starlike leaf.

"Well, that makes sense," he sarcastically muddled to himself but ultimately swallowed it.

It was not pleasant for him to have a raw, scratchy, sour salad like sensation twisting his face as he choked it down. Luckily from there, traveling through the forest was rather effortless for them.

"By the way, this ointment, I like it. Can I, have it?"

"By all means. But why do you keep calling me boy? I just turned nineteen! I am more than a boy now. I am a man!"

"When you have lived for two hundred years, then you can be a man."

"I suppose that is valid. So does that mean you are a witch or something? Uh, no offense."

"Hmm, I have been called something like that on more than one occasion, but no, I am a dragon."

"But how do you look human?"

"How do you look like a werewolf?" Echo said, mildly agitated by his forward questions. She continued by saying, "It is who I am."

Echo ignored Koldiar's many other questions when they arrived at the part of the cave where the ceiling dipped down.

"This narrow place is called Black territory. Who is Black? She is the one watching from the shadows. Her mouth salivates for your flesh. She is silence. She is the seven-foot-tall spider woman and self-proclaimed queen of the spiders, Lara Black."

"I have a small feeling we are being watched," Koldiar said. "That is because we are. They have been watching us for a while now."

"They? Who is they?" he asked.

"Lara and her children. Keep looking straight and stay calm," Echo said.

Small beads of sweat danced on both of their foreheads as they walked confidently into enemy territory. It was quiet until a small "Ssst!" disrupted it. What followed that noise were three grape-fruit-sized spiders descending from their line of webs. "Ssst! Ssst! Ssst!" They all went.

"Walk faster," said Echo as her pace steadily grew.

The faster they walked, the greater the number of spiders that descended in their path. Koldiar and Echo's anxiety spiked when their "fast walking" turned into an all-out run. The wall of spiders became thick like mud, and a river of arachnids gushed toward them from behind. It was not until they were surrounded by webs, they realized they could not run any longer.

"Hmm…darling, what are you doing here? Oh, have you come to apologize to me, hmm? Or have you come to finish me off? Hmm, that cannot be it. Your large…presence cannot possibly fit down here. So tell me why you are here! Is it to finally give yourself the death you deserve, hmm? I mean, especially with what you did to your brother." Lara chortled, lurking just past all the dense webbing that covered the trees.

"Lara, let us by. We just want passage through," Echo said. "Oh no no no no *no*, you do not command me in my own home! We have been here a lot longer than you or those damned pixies! Just for you to drive us into the narrows makes me dream of bleeding you dry and using your bones as decoration. However, I digress. I will be willing to let you pass if you only kneel before me. Oh, and with a smile, please."

Lara's words stabbed Echo's pride in the gut, and for a split second, she considered letting them have Koldiar as a peace offering. Even if she had, they would not have let her leave without a fight. Therefore, as for her next move, she had no choice but to kneel.

"I do not see a smile!" Lara said, revealing herself as an otherwise beautiful, gray-skinned, succubus of a spider woman. "Good, good, now call me your queen just once."

Echo's teeth clenched so hard she could have bitten through solid metal.

"M-My q-queen…" Those words pleased Lara to her core—so much so she broke out into a cackle.

"Thank you. Hmm, you may pass now." Lara "ssst" in pleasure. "Lara, it is always a delight. Come on!" Echo said, trying to

grasp at Koldiar's hand.

Although when she grasped a second time, she turned around to see him completely cocooned in webs and being dragged away.

"Lara! We had a deal!" Echo shouted.

"Oh, honey, I honored our deal. But maybe you should have included your friend in it as well."

This particular spider woman had a very talented tongue, and to make matters worse, her petty antic seemed to always beg her to play with her food. As Lara reveled in watching her children drag Koldiar into a hole, her elongated smile and obnoxious cackle fueled Echo's wrath.

Echo's blood boiled just at the thought of being bested by the likes of Lara. Although her trembling rage had her ready to kill everyone there, her weak human form could not do it.

This is it. Lara won. It is not like I know him. Oh well, wait, this looks familiar. Obsidian… These were all the thoughts that cluttered her mind when her mouth bargained for another deal.

"Lara, wait, make another deal with me!" These were only magic words that would always spark Ms. Black's interest.

"What is it you have to give, hmm? For this boy, it could not be much."

"Let him leave and let him live. And you can have me."

"You must be joking. For him? Well, your noose, your life," Lara said, allowing Echo to rip the silk webs at Koldiar's cocoon, letting his lungs snatch fresh air with a deep breath.

Echo quickly told him, "You have to leave now! Go past these trees and through the river, and the exit is there."

"Stop. They will kill you," said Koldiar. "Yes, I know."

She then backed away and, with a wince, let the immediate swarm of spiders wrap her body in her own personally spun coffin.

CHAPTER 11

Choices with a Quickness

Koldiar hobbled to the nearest tree after he tore through the rest of the webs that bound him. At first, he used the tree to help him stand, but when he looked back and saw Echo being dragged away, the raging wolf inside him howled. His heart began to pound, and beads of sweat started to swell on his forehead. His mind was falling into utter mania again.

He closed his eyes and said his thoughts aloud. "How could she do this? Why would she do this? She does not deserve this! Sorry but I am not leaving you!"

When his eyes opened, they were completely bloodshot. His nails grew and clenched through the bark of the tree. In his channeled fury, he uprooted the tree and threw it at the swarm of spiders, stopping them from dragging Echo away.

He then leaped over to her and ripped her from her coffin as she once did for him, and with a graveled voice, Koldiar yelled, "Come on, I am getting you out of here!"

He did not even wait for her to respond before grabbing her from her webbed shell and slinging her over his shoulder.

"You do know I can run on my own?" she said. Koldiar just kept running in silence.

"Uh, your grip is a bit tight there, boy." His grip only got tighter, and Echo continued, "Ugh, oh God! Let go. Let. Me. Go!"

She struggled to break free but unintentionally puffed a cloud of fire out of her mouth. Just as she realized she could use some of her abilities, she and Koldiar fell through a hidden spider burrow—Lara's secret tunnel system barely lit by the peeking glow of the roots above. She and her children had been building the burrows for months in order to surprise the pixies as they slept. Echo and Koldiar's thud was harsh as they dropped into the tunnels riddled with strands of webs and globs of rotten spider pods. Incidentally, when they fell through this hole of horrors, Echo landed on Koldiar, and Koldiar landed on his face.

Echo crawled off him to see if he was okay, and when she saw him breathing, she took a moment to stare at his still masculinity, thinking about how his bravery saved her. She was captivated by Koldiar, completely captivated.

When she touched his face with her silky fingertips, he awakened with a burst of confusion. "Whoa! Where am I? What happened?"

"Get up! They are coming. Follow me!" she said.

Her words were more motivating than watching an army of flesh-hungry arachnids crackling down a soggy tunnel. They quickly ran through the first tunnel they saw, following it as far as they could. The farther they ran, the denser the goopy thick webs became. Before they knew it, they had been trapped in webs too sticky to run through. "Hmm, nowhere to go? What a shame. Shame, shame, shame, shame!" Lara said, creeping from the shadows. They were trapped, at

least until Echo had an idea. "Boy, get down!" she yelled. "W-What?"

"Just do it! Have some faith," she said as she huddled over him like a mama duck to her hatchlings.

On Koldiar's back, he felt the most unbearable burning sensation. Echo had transformed herself back into the great crystal dragon she once was. In doing so, she breached her way out of the tunnel to the surface. Echo grabbed Koldiar with her talons and swiftly climbed out into the cramped shallows.

The instant they were out, Echo focused all her attention on the breach she made. There she waited and watched.

"Um…what are you doing?" "Shush!"

The moment Echo saw the first beady-eyed spider, Koldiar watched as a light shined from the tip of her tail. He then watched as the light coursed up the peaks of her spine and swelled in her belly. This light seemed to swirl rapidly before inflating her chest. What spewed out of her throat was the most incredible glistening blue flame. The flames ignited every part of that tunnel system. She set ablaze all of their eight-legged pursuers, seemingly leaving all spiders either dead or running in fear.

Echo and Koldiar fled the Narrows to the end of the cave called the Rounded River. This meant Echo and Koldiar must cross an unusually wide river that wrapped around the cave's only exit. The water was brisk and gentle; the mud made the most satisfyingly squishy feeling between their toes. It was a common interest they both shared—an immensely refreshing change for both of them considering all the happenings they just endured. They could not help but smile and chuckle to themselves.

Halfway through the shallow river, Koldiar said, "Koldiar." "Hm?" she said.

"My name…is Koldiar. I never introduced myself. What is yours?" he said.

"It is Echo," she said.

"You do not have a surname?" he said. "Do you?" she replied.

"Neir, Koldiar Neir."

"Well, Neir, Koldiar Neir, you may just call me Echo," she said. "Echo, if you do not mind my asking, why do you stay in a

place like this? Surely you could go anywhere you wished," he said. "I do!" Echo replied tersely, only to continue, "Nevertheless,

If you must ask, all my presence does is cause pain and torment. I deserve not to leave this cave," she said, darkening the mood.

"That sounds like you made this place a prison rather than your home. There is no way you can be deserving of a life like this, especially with the way you saved me," he said.

"Yes, that is true. Only because I lead you down that path. That is why I had no qualms about sacrificing myself. I was not going to allow another person to die because of me," she said.

"After terrorizing the city a few times and eating a few things that were not meant to be eaten, I should probably be the one locked away as well," he said before a short gloomy silence shrouded them as they waded through the river.

Words were not spoken, but you could hear their thoughts clear as day.

Koldiar glanced over at Echo to see her dreary expression, and he continued, "Like a skunk… That was not my best meals."

Echo struggled as she refrained from cracking a smile. He splashed her exposed legs to try and pull that smile of hers out but to no array, though he was close. He splashed a second time; this one was big enough to touch her cheek but still no smile. Koldiar was discouraged for sure.

Echo did not let any of Koldiar's splashes go unpunished; she retaliated by summoning her tail, swatting a sizable wave in his direction.

"Okay, I give up," he gargled as Echo finally smiled, and not only that but a laugh—a genuine laugh that grew louder even though Koldiar was less than amused.

He could tell this was the first laugh she has had in a long time.

To him, that made her even more beautiful than she already was.

When they arrived at the beginning of the exit tunnel, Koldiar asked, "Can we wait here a moment and dry off?" still completely drenched.

"Hmm, very well, I guess I could use a break," she playfully said, walking ahead of him to start a fire.

Koldiar sat in front of the fire she made from dead gray live branches. Echo and Koldiar sat back-to-back as he dried his clothes.

"Why do I need to look away again?" she said.

"Because you looking at me while I am naked makes me uncomfortable!" he said.

"If it is only because you are naked, I can be naked, too, if that makes you feel—" she said before Koldiar cut her off.

"No! No, that would be worse. Just give me a minute, okay?" he said.

"Okay, then hurry up. Pfft, humans," she said under her breath.

When Koldiar put on his dry warm clothes, he asked Echo, "So was it your brother you lost? I heard the spider lady talk about him." "Yes, and she knows that if I had done more, he would still be here," she said, lightly clenching her arm. "What happened?" he said.

"It is not something I want to—" "I apologize. You need not tell."

"It is fine. Just after our mother passed away, my younger brother went down a path I could have stopped…I should have stopped.

Ultimately, that path caught him between the path he wanted and a hideous monster. I chose to fix things to help him, but it was too late. His tail was severed, and his body died. Ever since, I have been hiding myself here like the monster I am."

"You are not a monster! It sounds like you loved your brother, and I am sure he does not blame you. You did what you could, and sometimes, things we cannot control happen. Honestly, I would love to have someone like you looking after me. Your brother was lucky," he said.

"You are sweet, but I doubt it," she said.

"Seriously! If you want, I could stay, and we can look after each—" Koldiar said while turning around to notice a small spider plunging its fangs deep into Echo's neck.

He smacked it off her and stomped it out, but it was too late for her. The potent venom was already coursing through her veins. Dragons, if you have not realized, are at their most vulnerable when in their camouflaged form. To make matters even worse, all dragons (with the exception of green dragons) are highly allergic to a spider's venom no matter how little. This meant Echo was on the verge of dying; she lost consciousness as she violently convulsed.

"Echo! Echo!" cried Koldiar.

"Take me…to the…pixies," she said, gathering all her strength to point beyond the trees to the deepest part of the cave.

Without a moment to waste, he placed her on his back and raced off as fast as he could. This man was on a mission; his grasp on her legs were strong and secure. He ran so fast that no footprints were left behind. The passion in his eyes let him see every leaf, root, and branch around him. Large ditches were nothing for his mighty legs to leap over. He had no time to be amazed that he ran two miles clear across the cave under eight minutes and jumped a thirty-foot ditch without even thinking. All he knew was that he had to save this woman.

Before he knew it, he began to hear talking and laughing; at last, he found the pixie's village.

"Someone, please help!" he shouted, completely rattling their entire dinner.

Everyone was apprehensive about approaching him until Syric shouted, "Koldiar? Guys, Koldiar is here!"

"Please, she was poisoned by Lara. She needs help," Koldiar said, showing her face.

"It is Echo!" Fonfon said before it was widely repeated by the whole crowd.

"Follow me and hurry! Fonfon, grab my medicines from my hut and then meet me at Molokai!" Lady Glady directed, thankfully taking charge of the situation.

He followed her to a smaller cave within the wall behind their village. This place was called Molokai—a perfectly circular pool of water with bright roots weaving the edges like a basket. The part that made this pool special was the indirect light shining down a hole of shiny crystals from the top of the mountain above them.

Glady directed Koldiar to rest Echo's head in the pool, making her hair spread out wildly. Fonfon arrived moments after with a basket of medicines.

While Glady picked through them, she instructed, "Son, now rest your head at the other end of the pool as well." She continued picking through her basket. "No, not that one. No, no, that is for lamp skin. Ah, spider antidote, okay, now come here, love." Lady Glady dabbed the antidote on her finger to rub on the infected area.

When Glady saw Koldiar's worried face, she said, "No need to fret, honey, just relax. So long as both of you are in the pool, everything will be fine. Our Molokai has mercy on the living so long as someone is willing to support that other's life with theirs. Molokai will balance the difference and give you both life." She muttered to herself after, "Although this is usually done through marriage but…"

"What was that?" he said.

"Nothing, just stay still. I am about to begin the ceremonial song," Glady said as she began humming loudly, which made Koldiar exceedingly more nervous.

Still, he was determined to save Echo no matter the cost. When Lady Glady was finished, Echo still did not move.

"You can get up now," said Glady.

"But what about Echo? She is still asleep!" he asked.

"Just relax, she just needs some rest now. Go, go eat something. You look hungry."

Koldiar reluctantly left Echo to Glady and went to eat. He then reunited with the rest of his Wisemen, who were all relieved to see him, though they had many questions to ask.

"How did you survive the fall?" "How did you get here?"

"Who was that striking young maiden?"

All of these questions were valid with the most valid one being, "Have you seen an exit?"

And for that, too, he had an answer.

CHAPTER 12

Taken

After a few bowls of stew, Koldiar had everyone eat a leaf to cancel out any more complications caused by the trees.

Thankfully, the two-mile hike back to the exit was a fairly easy walk. Still, the idea of a possibly charred spider queen alive and eager for revenge did not instill Koldiar with much confidence about leaving. Then the thought of Echo being in danger urged his heart to stay.

As Koldiar showed Orien, Fuzen, and Syric the way, they refrained from telling Koldiar that they found the tail. They sensed his moral hesitation and feared he may try to take the tail back to his lady friend, Echo. In the future time to come, Orien's only excuse for their secrecy will be, why you bringing up old business? You know what you would have done!

Koldiar also refrained from telling the part about Echo being the dragon they were looking for. For obvious reasons, they would have tried to hunt and hurt her. Though he was not so much worried they could kill her, he was more scared she would destroy them.

Through the rounded river, past the smoldering fire Echo started for him, and up the tunnel exit, they followed the trail up through the wet and rocky tunnel. This led them to the cave entrance hidden by a mossy veil. They pushed through the mossy curtain to after seeing the sun set before them a weight lifted from their shoulders as a fresh smell of relief let them breathe at ease. All of the Wisemen felt this relief except Koldiar.

Koldiar thought about all the mornings he had awakened, not having anyone to wake up for and no one to care for him. Thoughts about how maybe that was why he always wanted to be a Hayah holy knight for King Fayos or why he tries so hard to control himself. Although Koldiar was ignorant of what faith was, he unintentionally exerted a little faith when he decided his next move.

He stopped in his tracks to declare, "I'm going to stay here. That woman in that cave needs me, and I want to be there for her!" "No, you are coming with us," Orien said in a very agitated tone.

"Orien, do you all really even need me? You all did pretty well without me!"

"Oh, I care little if you leave, but they may have a problem with it."

Above them was a pack of more than a dozen Gaffmonkeys or the politically correct term, Wikas, which were cheap little mercenary hairballs known for rubbing their victims in poison ivy, an utter mistake in repugnant genetic history having half their ancestors being hairy gremlin and the other being crazed bald ogre. What they lack in mental fortitude, they make up in their sheer greedy nature. If it sounds as if people are particularly prejudiced or otherwise biased toward these brainless miscreants, then you would be right.

There they stood surrounded by a dozen Gaffmonkeys all pointing their crossbows at them. The clicking of their dirty weapons should have silenced any thought of escape. However, Syric thought for some reason they still had a chance of winning the fight (he still does to this day).

"All right, the five on the left are mine. I just need someone to—" Syric said, unsheathing his dagger.

"If you start fighting again, we are not helping," said Fuzen. "Why! We can take them!" Syric said, flinging his dagger around.

"Should I list the problems alphabetically, or should I just count how many Wikas there are," Fuzen said sarcastically.

"There are only twelve!" Syric exclaimed.

"Did you count the fourteen behind the bushes?" asked Orien. "Oh." Syric realized that they were a bit more outnumbered than he thought. He continued by saying, "Nah, we are doomed…" From that point on, the Wisemen were immediately shackled and roped together. As they were being transported to Jehovah-Knows-Where, they were serenaded by the maddening chant "Wika wahhh rrraaahh" for multiple hours to come. Despite the repetitive noise, Koldiar watched as the mauve sun hid itself behind the trees; he could not help but think about Echo's beauty and if she had awakened yet.

■■■

She did, in fact, wake up, and when she did, she asked, "Where am I? What happened!?"

"Echo! Calm down. Everything is okay! You are in the village," Fonfon said, watching over her.

"How did I get here?"

"That boy Koldiar brought you to the Molokai after a Sath spider bit you."

"The Molokai? Why there? I thought that was a holy ritual place…for couples."

"Uh, well, about that… Promise you will stay calm." Fonfon spoke reluctantly.

"I make no such promise," Echo said, already prepared to be angry with a worried wrinkle between her brow.

"Well, you see, when Lady Glady saw you, you were practically dead, so she had to…"

"Had to what?"

"Bond your life with that Koldiar's…?" Fonfon said rather softly.

"Meaning?" asked Echo.

Then Lady Glady flew to her and said, "Darling, this means both you and that boy's life forces are balanced—"

"And who told you to do that!" Echo shouted in disdain.

"I just—" Lady Glady shuddered.

"No! No one gave you the right! How dare you! You should have just let me die!" Echo stomped about.

"Darling, you have to understand, as long as one of you are alive, the other one will be as well. It was a good thing! Just a simple marriage ceremony so that you could live."

"M-Marriage!" Echo shouted angrily, stunned, and slowly turning red.

If you think her bursts of anger stopped there, then you would be surprised to know that a handful of pixie huts were burned down before she stormed off. Echo ran to the only place she could think of—the ruins where she kept her tail.

Before she entered the chamber where the tail should reside, Fonfon caught up to her, saying, "Echo! Hey, sorry about Lady Glady. We just really love you, and believe it or not, we just want you to be alive and happy."

"No, I should be the one apologizing. I should not have lost my temper with your grandmother like that."

"And burning her house down?" baited Fonfon.

"Eh, that part was actually pretty funny. But yes, I apologize for that too."

"No need, I thought it was pretty funny too. But look at the bright side, your husband is quite handsome."

"He is an idiot too," she said warmly, looking down as her feelings for Koldiar changed.

As she looked down, Echo saw a trail of dirt leading into the tail's chamber. Echo never tracked dirt into her chamber; therefore, it was highly suspicious.

Thunder struck when she opened the door, and her slight smile faded to a busheling thorn patch of rage. Echo's desperation consumed her very being. Her thorny vines frantically weaved throughout every nook and cranny of the musty room. Her once vibrant rose petals had now withered into dark pale chips. She painfully wept, hugging the pedestal that once held her heart. In that moment, a glimpse of Koldiar's smiling face struck a nerve. Echo's grip tightened, and her sharp claws dug into the crumbling stone brick until it was crushed by her scorn and consternation.

Echo, the dragon of the blue flame, exploded from the roof of the ruins and pounced toward the exit Koldiar was shown. Trees were obliterated just from the gust of her wings. Just one thing to note, it was not normal to see a dragon lose its mind in such a manner; it was absolutely unheard of. Like a mother searching for her young, Echo was no different.

When she made it to the exit, she scraped and clawed through the hole she was obviously too large for. Instead of transforming into her human body, she instead created a larger hole. Echo expelled the hottest blue flame she could muster that melted the sides of the tunnel, allowing her to squeeze through.

Sweltering cobblestone dripped from Echo's scales as she took to the crying sky. She set everything she thought was Koldiar on fire. She only realized he must have gotten away when the whole mountain was ablazed, and all she heard was the sizzling crackling pop of the rain hitting the trees.

In her anguish, she let out the most heart-wrenching, repetitive roar that screamed blue fire like a lighthouse into the melting night. Her flame was a beacon begging Koldiar to return what he had stolen.

All her feelings had connected to Koldiar; he could think of nothing, but Echo and he could feel her pain. This left his heart more weathered than the crunching gravel he walked over. Even from miles away, he heard the shatter of her breaking heart. Staggering under the weight of her emotion, the Wikas with a primitive spear probing his back reminded him that rest was not an option.

The Wisemen all huddled toward the unknown. Being pulled by horses, they slipped and stumbled, trying to keep up with one another, ultimately angering the Wikas further.

"Wahhnananahhhh kaaaaah!" screamed the largest of the little fluff demons. The only assumptions they had was to move faster.

Waiting for Koldiar, Orien, Syric, and Fuzen was a horse-drawn cage carriage parked on the road trail just before the thick forest. Koldiar looked back to the one thing his heart felt could never be obtained, only seeing a small blue streak of Echo's passion lighting up the night sky. This relieved him knowing she had survived, but he still could not help feeling deeply concerned for her.

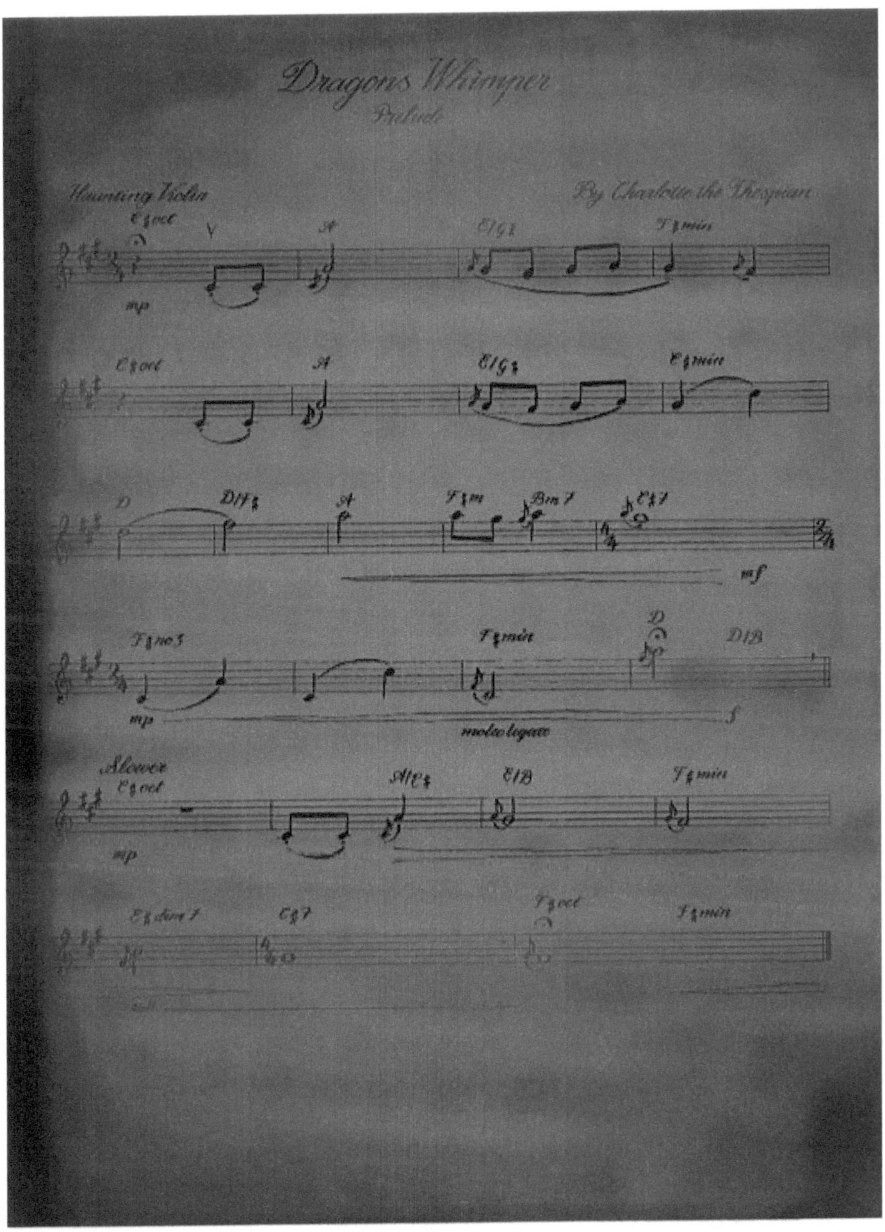
Dragon's Whimper
Prelude
Hunting Violin
By Charlotte the Thespian
Slower
molto legato
mp
mf
f
rall.

CHAPTER 13

Studying through the Window

This is an important part of the story that must be told before this tale goes any further (no if, ands, or buts about it). I must take you back to the beginning so that we can go forward.

Let's start with Princess Ismiellia and what role she plays in this tale. Ever since she heard of her father's absurd fables, she had been skeptical at best, especially after knowing what he planned to do after them. Talking to her father was practically useless; he was just too excited to listen to anything rational. Speaking of irrational, the morning after the festival, King Fayos ordered his artists to paint a mural of the dragon in his dreams.

That was the day Ismiellia knew she had to take matters into her own hands. To calm King Fayos's unhealthy addiction and put a stop to his foolish fables, Princess Ismiellia marched through the corridor to confront him yet again. In her haste, she ran into a gangly-looking man that looked as though he should not be within the castle's walls. He wore the royal colors on his doublet, but his face was still unknown, and the fact he was walking with entitlement bothered her to no end. She then took it upon herself to follow him all the way to the throne room where the king was having counsel with Victor Stow.

"So you mean to tell me that three random men snuck in the castle with half a dozen guards on the roof, five siren hounds circling the castle, and more than a dozen guards patrolling inside? Not to mention slipping past one hex rune to steal one item. Then out of all the gold and jewels you were specifically charged with guarding; they stole my grandmother's lullaby box."

"I see how it sounds, and honestly, I am just as shocked as you are, My Lord," said Victor Stow.

"Grant me one good reason why I should not make a vivid example out of you."

"My Lord, the great King Christopher Fayos, I beseech thee to spare this mound of orc filth!" begged Thespis.

"Thespis, my friend, why do you defend him?"

"Defend him? No, never! I merely mean to open thine eyes to the possibilities of using this man to acquire your dragon tail. If he is to succeed, then he may live, but if he does not, our only assumption can be…the dragon consumed him."

"Hmm, you make a powerful point. Let us try it your way and see how well you fare as my latest advisor."

"Advisor!" Ismiellia shouted.

"Oh, Ismiellia, you are awake quite early. Come, meet my newest advisor, Sir Thespis."

"Art thou as fair as a budding sage rose?" "Uh, yeah, pleasure."

"He was the one that wrote those lovely poems I showed you." "But, Father, what happened to Marren Pace? The Pace family have always been our advisors, even in times of old!"

"I am aware, but Marren Pace has proven to be untrustworthy. Apparently, there were plans to overthrow me, but with the help of Sir Thespis, I was able to act and dispose of him."

"Father, what have you done?" "What had to be done."

Ismiellia could not bear to think of what her father did, or rather what his new "advisor" convinced him to do. She stormed out of the throne room and straight to her room, trying not to shed a tear.

Although Ismiellia had been groomed to handle change at its most extreme, she was lost for answers. She had no thought as to how to fix the sinking ship she knew she was in until Ismiellia had an idea; she thought that maybe the only way to help her father was to leave the inner city of Wallacgrum to see this tail for herself and destroy it. Of course, that means if the tail does not destroy her first. Ismiellia had no idea what she was doing, or if she could be dooming her father more in the process.

Her journey found her caught between a giga-troll and a large mountain. Ismiellia had a hard decision to make. On one hand, her father could live out the rest of his short life like the strong king he has always been. But on the other hand, if the tail is real, he could receive this tail and suffer consequences worse than the black cough. Indeed a hard decision, one she decided was going to be made after gathering more information on dragons…and Sir Thespis.

But first, there was a minor mental meltdown that occurred in a corner of Ismiellia's chambers in front of her ivory vanity. She drove herself mad trying to talk herself out of leaving, crying, pretending to be brave, screaming into her pillow, and then crying some more. She felt a tad bit emotional when she realized the fact she must first leave the castle walls to get the information she needed. Also, the only one who could stand up to King Fayos and truly save him was her. Ismiellia came to realize many things about herself that morning, like due to her dislike of things unknown, she had never actually been outside the kingdom's walls before. All of her confidence was tailored to the kingdom and only to the kingdom.

Even though she calmed down when her handmaiden, Elizabeth, who was also her most favored confidant, let herself inside the slewing catastrophe that was her room. Elizabeth was there to do her scheduled check-ins, but even with her presence, Ismiellia's neurotic antics did not cease.

"Um, Princess, are you okay? I heard screaming from the hallway. What is wrong? Are you okay?"

"I do not know what to do! I just know my father is making a huge mistake, and I am the only one that sees past his idiotic plan. I just…I just need your help."

"Okay! Let me put some tea on first, or would you like some chocolate? How about cookies? The chef just created something he calls frozen milk. I was unsure about it, but it is actually quite goo—" "I need you to take me to the school of scholars in Grizona,"

Ismiellia demanded.

"Grizona! What kind of—no! For one, you need to be a witch or wizard. Secondly, do you want me to be strung up by my thumbs and beaten to death? Because that is what will happen…to both of us!" Elizabeth said shrilly.

"Elizabeth, you know a little bit of magic. It should not be too hard to blend in—"

"I was homeschooled! They will notice!" Elizabeth shouted.

"I am not telling you to perform a magic show! I just need you to pretend like you know what you are doing."

"I guess I can do that, but are you sure you want to do this? If we get caught snooping on Arcane grounds, there will be hell to pay," Elizabeth said, making it clear she still does not like Ismiellia's plan.

"I care not what happens to me, and I know it is a lot to ask of you, but I cannot stand idly by watching my father possibly destroy himself! I must learn more about dragons, so he does not learn the hard way."

"Fine, as you wish. I think I may have an idea, but we need robes." Elizabeth sighed before she scurried off to her quarters.

When she came back, she was holding two long brown-hooded robes in her arms.

"If Grizona is our destination, we will need to wear these." "These are all well and good, but how are we going to get there?"

Ismiellia asked.

"One thing at a time, please. As you know, my father was a professor that taught many things, and one of those things were dragons. I figure if the school had not cleared out his study yet, there should be plenty of scrolls about them," Elizabeth explained while guiding Ismiellia through the western ward corridors of the castle. She continued, "He also did plenty of work here teaching your father's Hayah Knights. So while doing two jobs extremely far away from each other, he made life easier by setting up a hidden way window in the castle."

"A way window?"

"A portal that connects to his study from the castle that should be somewhere over here…"

Elizabeth led Ismiellia down an old dead-end hallway that looked as if the maids had not dusted in a hundred years. Completely remote, Ismiellia was sure even her father was unaware of its existence. The floor was so unbelievably dusty they could follow the swept-over trail Elizabeth's father left behind. When Ismiellia saw where the trail led to, she was astounded to see that the way window was an actual window. A literal six-foot glass pane window that overlooked King Fayos's beloved royal glow bud garden.

"That window is a portal?" Ismiellia asked.

"Of course, what did you think a way window was?" "Um, not sure, but how do we use it?" Ismiellia asked. Elizabeth hiked up her dress, saying, "Just jump through!"

Elizabeth insisted before she ran and dove full force straight into the window, disappearing out of sight.

Ismiellia hesitated for a moment like any normal woman would, but when a guard at the end of the hallway yelled, "Who goes there?" She knew it was now or never.

She bolted through the glass just as Elizabeth did. Swirling and whirling in a rainbow kaleidoscope of existence, they fell only for an instant before colliding on top of a firm lounge of pillows. Lying in front of a window nook, they noticed they had indeed arrived within the walls of Grizona, within Professor Fuzen Waykin's personal study.

Even though the room was a basic boardroom, Ismiellia was still highly impressed by all the scrolls that covered every inch of his walls. Hundreds of scrolls were tastefully placed inside their own little individual mantle.

"Thank goodness nothing has been touched. Even his work slippers are still here," said Elizabeth.

"How do we know what scroll is for what? Why are there not any labels?" asked Ismiellia.

"Well, before a powerful wizard cursed my father's thoughts, he had an outstanding memory. He saw no need for labels."

"Does that mean we have to check all of the…?" Ismiellia reluctantly questioned.

"That means we have to check all of them," Elizabeth confirmed.

They both thought it would take hours before they would find the scroll they needed, and it did. Before they knew it, four hours had passed as the room quickly became a sty. Elizabeth had already been on break for two hours, but Ismiellia kept searching. She had never been more determined in her life, pulling out scroll after scroll; from medicinal potion recipes to the art of drawn spells, Fuzen had everything. Most of the scrolls taught how to enunciate magical spell sounds with proper diction. However, right outside the room, they heard a man talking; the closer his voice sounded, the more they both panicked.

"Ismi, I do not want to lose my thumbs!" Elizabeth loudly

whispered.

The door began to creak open, and a young sorcerer by the name Braynard Gini walked in with arms full of scrolls.

"Halt! What are you two doing in Professor Thespis's study?"

"What do you mean? This is Fuzen Waykin's study!" Ismiellia said, covering for Elizabeth.

"It was, before he lost his memory and was fired. Now Professor Thespis resides in this study."

Ismiellia was stunned to hear that name again. Could this be the same man that is advising my father? Ismiellia thought to herself as she continued to ask, "Thespis Oltrage?"

"So you heard of him? I would be surprised if he were not such a legendary man, especially after picking up Professor Fuzen's scheduled classes he failed to perform."

"What makes this man so legendary?"

"Where do I begin… From the royals he met and the places he has been, he is absolutely inspiring. He told us that once, he was stranded on a mountaintop for twenty-one days only to escape by plucking the feathers off a sleeping griffin and gliding down."

"Why not use magic?" asked Ismiellia, already believing that this Thespis man was an outstanding liar.

"Thespis is a kind man. He would never use magic to harm a griffin! Hold on, these are things we took a test on. Who are you two? "I am Elizabeth Waykin, and this is my sister, Ismi Waykin. Our father sent us here to find scrolls regarding dragons," Ismiellia said.

"Y-Your f-father! Outstanding, both of you must have just enrolled!" Braynard stuttered.

"In light of current dispositions, our father cannot teach us at home."

"I apologize for my rudeness. I am so very sorry about your father's memory loss… Oh, and the scrolls you spoke of, I have them right here."

"Thank you, but if you would be so kind, we must be on our way now."

"If I might, I recommend Harry Dalf's: How a Pirate Trained a Dragon. it is an absolutely outstanding short story from a talented traveling scholar."

"That sounds amazing. We will be sure to read it," Elizabeth said, juggling all the scrolls out of Braynard's hands.

"I shall leave you two to it. I must excuse myself, ladies. My next class is beginning shortly," he said, leaving Ismiellia and Elizabeth to their own devices.

However, after closing the door, Braynard realized he had accidentally lent them his family's lucky quill. He doubled back through the study door to obtain it only to find it was too late. Ismiellia and Elizabeth were gone.

Through the way window and after a narrow escape, both ladies were very pleased with themselves and giggled about it on their way back to Ismiellia's room.

"That was enough excitement for one day, and I am sure you want to study as much as you can. I hope it helps," Elizabeth exclaimed.

"Honestly, thank you. You have no idea know how much this means to me."

These are words that Ismiellia could not have said any more earnestly. The two parted ways when Ismiellia entered her chambers. Wasting little time, she dived into the many scrolls they acquired. Within Fuzen's four scrolls, he wrote information that focused on their classification and anatomy known as Alpha-Draco Chamaeleonidae— large reptilian creatures with scales tougher than the most advanced Dwarven armor, four-legged creatures having the strength of more than a dozen horses with tremendous batlike wings enabling them to fly two times faster than their ability to run.

There were many other basic features like tails, eyes, ears, mouths, but nothing of use. Yet after finding nothing going through Fuzen's class material, Ismiellia felt more lost than when she started her journey. That is until she ripped a section of the thirty-six-foot scroll paper and found that there were sheets pasted to the back of his work. She realized she did something good. Ismiellia had a momentary fear for what the wizards would do if they found out. However, when she felt the thickness of the paper that tore, she saw a part of the paper pasted underneath; she knew Fuzen was hiding something. Ismiellia could not pull the two sheets apart, but she found that if she held the paper in front of her candle, she could read the other side. The scriptures underneath spoke further in-depth about dragons. The text reads,

Through my journey of proficient renewal, I traveled across Railam and the nations beyond, but who would have believed I would find a dragon living among the people of Fasoom named Thespis Oltrage. He was just as much interested in wizards as I was with dragons; therefore, I taught him about wizards as he taught me about being an Alpha-Draco Chamaeleonidae. As fate would have it, dragons do share the same ability to breathe fire out their mouth but can have unique attributes depending on their subclass color. Out of the three species he came across—there were green, black, and blue dragons—green dragons, along with green fire, can breathe clouds of poisonous and corrosive gas. Blue dragons can breathe blue that can purify and cleanse any negative or evil intent. However, when it came to black dragon's breath attack, It was scratched out, and she read more.

Every time a dragon prepares for a breath attack, a small glow travels from the tip of their tail down the underbelly and then up out the mouth. It occurred to me that this is where they draw their power from—correction, I believe that is where their soul resides. If that be true, their flames are not completely biological but are some kind of magic.

He called it Thikun, which means "to change soul."

Along with their ability to breathe fire, they can use Thikun to transform at will. However, as Thespis described, their changed form is not without limitations, but after they reach pubescent age, it only allows them to morph into only one humanoid creature. It seems to be strictly for camouflage purposes, and it also seems to be just as vulnerable as whatever form they decide to change into.

She had it: proof that the foolish pursuit her father was hellbent on was a malevolent plot controlled by Thespis. Without hesitation, she snatched her scroll and marched to her throne room, ignoring everyone trying to talk to her on her way. When she barged through the castle corridor that led into the throne room, she stood in front of the man, no, the dragon, Sir Thespis.

"Lady of youth, pickling beauty! Enlighten me, what haste there be?"

"I need to speak to my father!" Ismiellia said, stunned as to why she even entertained his question.

"Tell me, ever what for?"

"I plan to spill the truth on your plot to seize the throne!" she said yet again reluctantly.

"Show me what proof you have," Thespis said.

Ismiellia knew she did not want to hand over the scroll, but something inside her went against her own will and was somehow forced to hand over the long sheet of Fuzen's hidden studies to Thespis.

Seeing nothing of this proof Ismiellia spoke of, he continued, "I see no proof! Explain! Where is this proof!"

"Fuzen was smarter than you gave him credit for. He hid his studies of you under his lessons!"

"Seems the sly fox shall rise from thine hen coop. A plague has already consumed thine father's mind. Thus, all ambitions thou con- jure, art folly!"

With the end of his words, three guards came out from the throne room.

"Is everything all right, Princess Ismiellia and Sir Thespis?" "No, Sir Thespis—" Ismiellia said before Thespis interrupted. "Was lamenting to dearest Princess to never disturb a king as he

sleeps. Take her to the dungeon!"

With that, the guards bound her arms and gagged her mouth and then carried her off to the farthest reaches of the dungeon to make sure no one would ever find her from the depths she was placed; not even a murderer should deserve to go where she went.

Before they left her in the dark, Ismiellia tried pleading, "M-m- m-m-m!" she mumbled and squirmed in her tout restraints, but it was useless; they walked away, and their lantern lights dissipated.

For hours, she was left to her own thoughts as grief smothered her like a dagger slowly piercing her side. She accepted the darkness. She accepted her restraints along with her cell, especially since she accepted that her father's fate was sealed. She felt powerless to stop it—powerless to stop his dragon that seemed more capable and more prepared, but in her dark, muggy dungeon, a latent fierceness lit the darkness. There arose two of her best qualities: a fearlessness that would define her for the rest of her life and a perseverance that would make her a tidal wave of power. She swore if she ever escaped, she would make Thespis pay.

Jehovah must have felt Ismiellia's determination because in the darkness, she saw a flicker of hope moving closer and closer toward her cell. She swore it was the guards, but no, it was her dear ally, Elizabeth, who had come to save her.

"Ismiellia, is that you! I saw what they did to you," she said, struggling to open the iron bar door.

Never did the sound of clanging metal and squeaking hinges sound sweeter for Ismiellia.

"Are you all right? Did they hurt you?" Elizabeth said while removing the restraints that muzzled Ismiellia's voice.

"Elizabeth! I am so glad to see you! No, I am unharmed. However, Thespis will not be able to say likewise when I get hold of him."

Both Ismiellia and Elizabeth snuck through the castle, through the servant's quarters within the bastion kitchen. This was where they hid until after the head chef prepared dinner and just before the morning cook prepared breakfast. This was by far the most discreet place to take refuge through the late night.

"No matter what, we must leave the castle before they realize you escaped," said Elizabeth, packing whatever food she found into her bag.

"I agree, but you cannot come with me. It is way too dangerous," Ismiellia added.

"How can I just leave you to fend for yourself!" Elizabeth said. "My father made sure I knew how to fight! Although fighting dragons was a lesson he thoroughly neglected. I am fully capable of
protecting myself. Moreover, you are with child."

"How did you know!" Elizabeth asked, shocked that no one figured out her secret.

"You have been glowing for the last month! You think I would not notice? Therefore, you have to stay here. Go back to your regular duties and keep your head down."

"Fine, but where will you go?"

"I will go to Agisshara and destroy that damned tail myself!" Ismiellia said, mostly to herself.

Those words served as a declaration from her heart, burning a brand on her spirit.

Ismiellia's strong will guide her out of the main kitchen. She was made privy as to the right time the late-night guards shifted their positions to the early morning guards. She hugged all the hidden nooks and crannies as she snuck all the way to the royal stable. Her original plan was to saddle a horse for the journey, but there was no way to do that without alerting tower guards. However, after she noticed Victor Stow packing a wagon by himself, there was an easier option she could take: the way of a stowaway.

"Please be careful, Ismi!" Elizabeth prayed; she sat worried in her servant's quarters.

The robe Ismiellia still wore looked indistinguishable from Victor's many brown gunny sacks that he tossed into his wagon. She stowed away while he loudly complained to himself about Orien, and before she knew it, they were off—off they went through the stonegated walls crowned with twisted weaved bars and into Ismiellia's new journey.

CHAPTER 14

Now that a very important piece of this tale has been told, we may go further with the troubles of Koldiar and his three deeply exhausted Wisemen. They all were forced to stay awake from the Gaffmonkeys' whippings with switches and the scolding drops of the night rain. Between being beaten through the open-barred cage and Fuzen's howl every time it happened, the only true relief on their journey was the rain clearing early that morning. Then all they had to deal with were the heat and the looming fact that they were being prepared for something heinous.

Although Koldiar and Fuzen were barely keeping their composure, Orien and Syric seemed nonchalant about the ordeal, playing games of Fus, roh, dah with their hands to pass the time. Koldiar would have been interested if he still had not felt somewhat guilty for leaving Echo. As for Fuzen, the term mad fails to describe this poor man's state of confusion. Fuzen was like a lunatic, continuously mumbling spells and scratching symbols into the metal floor and then laughing in despair when his runes failed.

Around the time Fuzen shouted out his last "spell," which still seemed pointless, all of the Wikas became enraged by his ruckus. With metal collars charmed with a symbol of suppression, the Wikas intentionally and efficiently silenced the whole carriage. Not a sound was made from that point further, not even to express the simplest groan. I was positive that if they had made another single sound, the Wikas would have personally sucked their eyes right from their sockets.

All the prisoners could do was watch and wait as they rode through the sweltering heat of the day. With no surprise, the hairy Wikas overheat far too easily, causing them to have to take breaks more often than not. For creatures with no sweat glands, they struggled a considerable amount in the humidity. In any case, you can only imagine how the guys felt in their metal cage with no water or shade. For someone that lived most his life in a treehouse, Koldiar suffered the most from the heat. Desperate and dehydrated, Koldiar was having frequent thoughts of whether or not he was hallucinating, especially when he saw Echo in a puddle made from his dripping forehead sweat.

Echo, in her human form, looking just as exhausted and oh so very somber. From a stream, she drank water cupped in her hands. Echo! he thought, but she just kept drinking. Echo! he thought louder, finally sparking her attention. She tenderly looked up at him, and through her reflection, she saw Koldiar in the waterfall. The fluidity of her diamond-like gaze fell like the water she washed her face in. From her disdain, his spirit crashed, and his soul drowned. Just by that one look, she sank his heart.

"I will never let you have his tail, thief! You knew it was all I had left of him, and you took him anyway! I promise I will find you, Koldiar, even if I have to hunt you down to the pits of hell!"

What are you talking about? What tail? I would never steal from you, I promise! he thought.

"Lies!" she yelled.

I swear, I am not! I was helping my lost friends leave the cave while you were resting. I had full intentions of coming back to you, he replied. "There were more of you? They must have stolen him while you distracted me. I will kill them all too," she said to herself.

With a fire reignited and a sense of his whereabouts, the woman on a mission transformed and took the sky. All of Koldiar's frustration peaked, and he attempted to slam his fist into the metal floor, but at that moment, Koldiar realized Fuzen's spells actually worked; Koldiar's fist fazed right through the floor.

The only problem, though—and it certainly was a problem—somehow, Fuzen managed to cast the spell on Koldiar and only Koldiar, allowing him to slip straight through the dense metal. This only attracted the attention of the shocked and woeful faces of his three foolish companions. Aside from being left behind, Koldiar was now a free man, but as good as this revelation was, he still did not want any of them to be maimed, murdered, or violated, especially when he could possibly help their situation. However, before he followed, he had to first unbuckle the charmed collar that silenced him. After the collar was ripped apart by Koldiar's barbaric brutality, he tried his best to track the wagon trail, but all his efforts were dashed as the sun began to set. The time was dusk, and Koldiar had realized that he passed the same mossy tree stump three times in a row. Normally, in any other circumstance, Koldiar's sense of direction would have been exceptional, but cloud of black flies, as they are called, nearly blinded him. Hundreds of them swarmed around, biting and stinging. Many of them were still babies with no stingers or teeth, but what they lacked in defensive ability they made up for by flying with full force into his eyes.

Even though his vision was otherwise obstructed, his sense of smell was still sharper than ever. The scent of burning bumble damp wood in the distance faintly reached his nose. In his mind, he thought, it has to be Orien, Fuzen, and Syric. Maybe I can save them!

He fled the best he could toward the possible campfire and away from the chasing swarm of black flies. Thankfully, the closer he walked, the more the black flies seemed to be warded off by the bumble damp smoke. Although the closer he traveled, the more the smells of roasted dates and chamomile lured him in. The smell was becoming much louder and more robust with a slight note of sunflowers seeping through.

Koldiar peeped through two shabby bushes to see an aged man sipping chamomile tea from a bowl and roasting his skewered dates as he gnawed on sunflower seeds. This man with seed shells scattered around his bare feet was a true hermit in his own right going so far as to build a hut in the middle of a treacherous forest, much further away from civilization than Koldiar ever wanted. Koldiar thought of all the warning signs while watching the old hermit; he opted against approaching him even though his dates smelled wonderful.

Despite Koldiar's stealth, the man knew he was there; in fact, he knew where everyone in the forest was. From the tiniest ant to the crystal dragon resting in the close distance, he could smell them all. With all of that in mind, it should come to no surprise that the old man exposed

Koldiar's presence.

"Boy, come out from the bushes. I care not for stalkers this time of night. If you are hungry, come and eat. I have no reason to harm you. On the contrary, I may be able to help you. You are trying to find your friends, right? I can point you in the right direction."

"You know what happened to them?" Koldiar said, brushing past the bushes he hid behind to face a man sitting on a rickety-weathered chair before a raging bonfire.

Only his hairy elongated arms and legs were visible due to his short, tattered robe.

"Nothing in this forest is hidden from my nose. I smelled you from the moment you entered my forest, and I could tell you were all imprisoned. One does not forget the smell of Gaffmonkeys. So I assume you would like to know where your friends are, and I can help."

"You would do that for me?" Koldiar asked.

"For a brotha, anything. But would you not do an old man a favor first?" the man asked.

"What would you need me to do?" he asked, seeming highly skeptical.

"Nothing too taxing. Just wash my weary feet," he said.

"Are you sure you want me to do that?" Koldiar asked reluctantly after seeing how unpleasant his deformed feet looked.

"Yes, to respect your elders, boy, is to wash their feet. Chance has it that my feet have been killing me all day. So if you are not willing to wash my feet, I am more than capable of washing them myself, just as you are capable of finding your friends alone," he threatened.

"Sorry, sir, I will wash them," Koldiar agreed.

"Anyway, the pail and soap are by my door. Please place it near the fire so it can warm up," he said.

"By the way, what do I call you?" Koldiar asked while trying not to spill the pail of water filled to the brim.

"You first. You are the stranger here after all." "Oh, sorry!"

"Stop being so damn sorry!"

"Uh, sor… My name is Koldiar Nier."

"Good, you can learn. It is a pleasure to meet you, my brotha. Many have called me by the slave name society has given me, Gad Morbliee, but out here, I am free to use my true Nubian name! Call me Ellex Aiden," he said, extending his hairy lanky hand out in greetings while revealing his half-wolf-formed face.

"Whoa! You are like me."

"Well, almost. A run-in with a dragon some time ago did this to me."

"A dragon did this to you?"

"Yes, and that was the most terrifying time in my life. Even in my other form, I froze when it roared, and when I failed to run away, it blazed me with its blue flame, and that is why I have this quasi form."

"So when I was dreaming, I saw your memories?" asked Koldiar. "We werewolves are all brothas, Koldiar, but we are not that connected. But it does sound like something is trying to grow your faith."

"I keep hearing about faith, but I have no idea what it means." "Faith is the body of things hoped for and the indication of things not seen," Ellex said, waiting for a response when he realized Koldiar still did not quite understand. Ellex continued, "I can see you are still lost. Let us try again. Imagine that you want to enter my home, but despite all your strength, you are still unable to break through my door. You want everything my home has to offer, and you believe that I, the owner of this house, will let you in. So you believe in me, and I finally grant you a key. That key is the symbol of your faith."

"So my belief is faith?" Koldiar asked.

"Exactly! Our faith is the key." Ellex applauded. "May I ask what it is you have faith for?"

"Throughout all my years, I have failed to find something that will cure this mutation we share, so I figured I would give up and believe in Jehovah. Maybe then I could be a normal man and one day perish pure. As I said, it is not an accident I am unable to fully morph. That dragon's fire somehow cures people like us. I just know it!"

Hmm, I wonder if he is talking about… Yes, it has to be Echo, he thought to himself and continued to ask, "I am finished. Do you mind helping me find my friends now?"

"Certainly. Since the moment you all arrived, it was very hard shaking the smell of gnome," Ellex said, sniffing the air. "Your friends are north of here, but you need not hurry. Seems as though they have stopped for the night. Feel free to sleep here if you like. Nothing should bother you so long as the fire burns. As for me, my brotha, I will bid you a good night."

With that, he tottered to his little hut and swiftly closed the door behind him. Koldiar's thoughts were swirling about what faith really means when, becoming a holy night, he lay there by the fire and ate a bit of Ellex's dates he left behind and thought until he had drifted further asleep than he wanted.

Early that morning, a loud crash jarred Koldiar awake.

"Where is it!" yelled a surly Echo upon Ellex's now half-demolished hut.

"What are you talking about!" yelled a confused Ellex. "I know you are hiding it from me!" Echo shouted.

Koldiar wiped the crumbs from his eyes to see Echo in dragon form glistening in the morning light, trying to claw Ellex out from his bedroom.

"Echo? Oh no!" Koldiar said to himself. "Give it back!" Echo continued to shout. "Echo! Stop!" cried Koldiar.

However, before he could get her attention, she attacked with her blue fire through the hole she created and burned Ellex alive.

"I can get your tail back!" The moment Koldiar shouted that, Echo's ears perked up, and she descended from the roof, transforming into her human form as she landed. She was not even fazed by the fact that she probably just murdered someone.

"Take me to it right now!"

"No! You probably just killed someone. I am going to check on him first."

"He should be fine."

"What do you mean he should be fi—"

"I am cured!" cheered Ellex, strolling out from his burning home with a big smile on his face.

Although his house was burning and his clothes were practically singed off, all that failed to matter since his body was not half-formed anymore. He was a completely normal man now, and he could not be happier about it.

Even when his body gave way to all the years he had lived, he smiled when he told Koldiar, "Koldiar, it seems my key worked. Thank you for your company." It was the last thing he said, finally at peace before he aged into a pile of bones.

"Hmm, maybe not as fine as I thought," Echo questioned herself.

"You killed him."

"I did not kill him. Time killed him. I just unintentionally helped."

"By shooting him with fire?"

"First of all, mind your tongue with me. You are still on thin ice. Secondly, my flames only harm those with vile hearts and wicked intent."

"He was a good man, though!"

"Well, apparently, I have the ability to fix people like you. I really was not trying to kill him."

Koldiar looked at Echo, and before he could ask his next question, Echo beat him with her answer.

"No, it is not going to happen!"

"Come on, I told you I did not steal your tail—"

"Either you are stupid, or you think I am. Why would I ever believe you?"

"Because I was with you the whole time." "But your friends were not!"

"Hmm, yeah about them… They kind of got captured by Gaffmonkeys, so how about this, I will help your get your tail back if you help me rescue my friends."

"Hmm, and I suppose you want me to assist you with your werewolf problem as well, huh?"

"If you don't mind."

"Don't?" Echo vaguely repeated.

"Oh, it is something my friend says. It means 'do not,' just shorter."

"Maybe you are stupid," Echo mumbled to herself as she continued, "Anyway, my two stipulations are, you keep all your friends away from me, and you will pledge your allegiance to me until I received the tail."

"Very well, you have my word!"

With all things considered, this was probably the best outcome that could have transpired. The two of them trudged through yet another forest together. As they walked, Echo almost showed a small bit of sweetness when Koldiar caught her arm before she tripped over a hitched vine. Still, he was instantly met with a cold shoulder when their eyes met.

"Oh, um, would it not be faster if we flew to them?" "Would you proceed to treat a lion as a house cat?" "No?"

"Good, then you can understand that I am not a mount."

It was all too clear Echo was still not in the mood for him even though she had no real reason to be so short with him. All it took was a simple stomach gargle to realize what was wrong. Echo had been fiercely searching for him and had forgotten to eat. It happens to the best of us, even raging dragons.

"Are you hungry?" Koldiar asked.

"No," she said as her stomach gargled again. "Are you sure?"

"Please stop talking."

"Well, if you change your mind, you can have some of my dates," he said, untying the date-filled pouch from his rope belt.

Echo had planned not to partake in Koldiar's date, but when she smelled the fruity aroma, she glared at him and snatched the pouch from Koldiar's hand.

"Fine! I will eat them. Now leave me alone about it."

Koldiar quickly looked away and smirked as Echo discreetly shoved a handful into her mouth. The farther they walked, the less discreet her eating was, and the more she ate, the more relaxed she became.

"I am sorry about your friend back there. I had no idea that would happen."

"He was not my friend, but he was probably the only one that understood me. Hmm, his faith allowed him the peaceful passing he always wanted. So you don't have to be so sorry."

Echo just glanced at him as though she secretly wanted to admire him.

CHAPTER 15

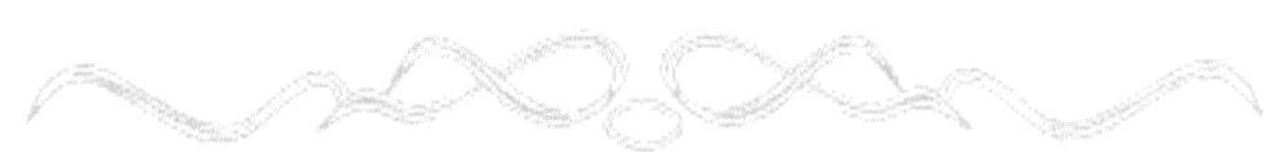

No, it is Mine!

Once again, Echo and Koldiar were alone trekking through the Stain forest together in the hopes of finding Orien, Fuzen, Syric, and the tail. They continued past the Gaffmonkeys' night camp and followed loose remnants of wadded clumps of Wika hair. One could tell Echo was becoming impatient, and that made Koldiar a bit anxious that she may leave off or worse lose her temper. Luckily, they followed the tracks just outside the Stain Forest to a meadow clearing where in the distance, both Echo and Koldiar watched as Orien, Fuzen, and Syric were being brought to a large convoy.

"This is not going to end well," Koldiar said while atop a hill, peering down through the long thick grass.

No, this will not end well at all, Syric thought as if responding to Koldiar's statement.

The convoy was stationed around the grand cherry blossom tree of Wallacgrum that was waving the infamous goat-eyed flag. If you knew anything about what the symbol of the goat-eyed flag represented, you would be on the verge of soiling your trousers, just as Orien was. This flag represents carnage with the vow to pillage, abolish, and destroy—to pillage from those who have more than them, to abolish the rules created by the noblemen, and to destroy the idea of safety.

This brotherhood of wickedness was known as the goat-eyed bandits. As I stated earlier, Orien lost most control of his bowels at the sight of their flag as it waved from a high branch on the grand cherry blossom tree. Orien frantically shook his bar doors, begging for freedom. Sadly, the only sound to convey his distress was a rapid clanking.

As Koldiar watched the usually calm Orien panicking, he thought of a plan.

"Okay, Echo, I will go down, find the tail, and when you hear my whistle, then you will come down and help me save my guys. Is that okay?" he timidly asked.

"Not sure of how I feel about the whole 'whistling part,' but I suppose I will play along," Echo agreed, knowing full well she was not going to follow his plan.

As time refused to remain stagnant, they watched and waited as the lead Wika let out a cry, alerting a familiar face to meet them as they pulled up.

"What a stupendous surprise! My 'friend' Orien Alexander Fike!" said by the relentless Victor Stow with a slimy smirk on his face.

"What? Unable to speak? Have you decided not to use that silver tongue of yours to come up with the perfect falsehood? Not like I would indulge you. Besides, after Her Highness is through with you, there will be little to listen to, anyway. Now, you four, strip them and prepare them for Ma'amela!" Victor said before waltzing over to the group of Wikas to award them for their services.

The Wikas were met with three large sacks stuffed with three of the most succulent salt-roasted hogs. It was quite sickening really to think that Gaffmonkeys highly preferred food as compensation instead of gold. More often than not, one could get a quick jolly for offering them a sandwich. As unconventional and gluttonous as they are, they are apt to do a job well.

After the Gaffmonkeys were paid, Victor ordered four of the crudest disguised bandits to strip Orien, Syric, and Fuzen off all their belongings, taking as much as they could, only leaving them with their memories. Granted, perhaps, that analogy was not as sensitive to Fuzen as it could have been, but they still made off with the lantern that held the tail, the golden lullaby box, the diamonds, and all their weapons. However, while the bandits were thoroughly searching them, one seemed dainty and uncomfortable. Even though her face was being covered, she did not seem to act as the others did.

Nevertheless, Orien, Syric, and Fuzen were all violently dragged in the middle of the convoy and strapped to wooden spokes. Before them was a crackling hot hog roasting over a firepit. The tiny embers snapped at their feet as they gazed past the bonfire. There was one large tent that stood differently than the rest; it looked somewhat more important than the others did. As soon as they were securely tied, all the bandits left from their respective tents to gather around them. Giddy with excitement, all the bandits waited for their incredibly special leader to grace them with her presence.

After the Gaffmoney left with their spoils and the bandit waited for their leader, Koldiar was able to sneak his way into the camp. He found the bench where all of Orien's belongings were placed, but before he could find the tail, a bandit woman stopped him. With the sharp point of her dagger pressed in his back, Koldiar froze.

"Hands where I can see them!" the woman commanded.

"Oh, okay…okay," he muttered, complying with her demands.

For a moment, she stared at him as if she saw a ghost until she fearfully asked, "Koldiar?"

He was too confused to respond and almost too scared to reply.

The only reaction he gave was a befuddled look.

"It has to be you! You are the only one that could give such a stupid look."

"Who are you?" Koldiar asked, even more confused than he already was.

She did not say a word. All she did was remove the bandages from her face to show a faded scar from above her left ear to the bottom of her jaw. Again, he did not know what to say. Honestly, what could he say?

"Koldiar, that hurts. I know it has been years, but if you are going to give your best friend a scar, at least remember it."

"Ismiellia? Ismiellia!" Koldiar said as his face began to light up.

"Sssh!" Ismiellia shushed.

"How are—wait, hold on! Why are you here!?" he whispered loudly.

"I could ask you the same thing!"

"It is a very a long story, but right now, the fact of the matter is that I came here to save my friends and return the dragon tail they stole."

"The tail…they found the tail? Listen to me, Koldiar. That tail is evil! It must be destroyed! My father will stop at nothing until he finds it! Oh, Ma'amela is coming out. Hide! I will go to look around to see if I can find it, but please, you must help me destroy it, Koldiar!"

Before Koldiar could say another word, she ran off. Fixing her bandages, she blended back into the masses gathering around Orien, Syric, and Fuzen. Staggered by this conflicting request, Koldiar was left, yet again, lost for words as the crowd of bandits started to beat their brass drums for the appearance of their leader.

Scurrying out of the largest tent were two slaves wearing nothing but trousers as they held the tent shroud open. Two more slaves scampered out quickly, crawling on their hands and knees. Lastly, in all her glory, out of the tent waddled a bark-skinned wood elf. This was Ma'amela—a grossly overweight female, better known in elf culture as a Divera. In her ivory silk nightgown, Ma'amela adorned herself in gold rings, bands, and tasseled earrings. This impossible Divera wore her shiny black hair in the shape of a beehive. Her bulbous beehive was embellished with what she called sapling curls, which reached down to cover her bulging cheeks.

Ma'amela hobbled out and unleashed the full load of all her weight upon her two scrawny slaves. It was highly likely that those poor slaves cried during this whole process. The two slaves that had held the shroud open for her were not exempt from work either; they supported her back.

As she comfortably snuggled into her half-naked slave chair, she said, "Every time I come out here, ya got a problem! Honestly, ya act like some damn fools! Someone needs to tell me who these people are?"

"This man stole from us, Mum! Got me fired from my position guarding the vault, and the others are his accomplices," Victor replied as Ma'amela turned her gaze to Orien.

"Oh, Orien Fike! How I have missed you…with my arrows. So you think you can make us look weak and get away with it? I worked too hard for this to let one demiling make a fool out of us! Bring me their things!"

One of her slaves supporting her back ran off and brought back all their items.

"It is nice to see you still have our golden box, and oh, what is this? No…is this that tail king flathead wants so badly? Oh ho ho, I am proud of all of you! You have done the impossible. Now do you have any last words before I let my scorpions scrap out the balls of your eyes?"

Orien just looked at her with the fear of God in the balls of his eyes.

"Boy, you betta answer me when I talk to you," she said. Noticing his silencing necklace, she gritted her teeth with extreme annoyance.

"Victor," she called. "Yes, Mum?"

"Take those necklaces off them!" she shouted, clenching her teeth.

With a quickness, he scrambled his way over to Orien, Fuzen, and Syric, relieving them of their necklaces.

"Sorry, Mum, sorry," Victor said as he disappeared from Ma'amela's glare.

After Orien's voice returned, she asked him again, "What do you have to say for ya actions?"

With a straight face, he looked her in the eyes and said, "Not apologizing."

"What?" she said, genuinely not hearing him.

"I am not apologizing! You are just mad because your mother introduced you to oiled chicken, and now you are fat because of it!"

Ma'amela gasped, and for a moment, everyone refused to make a sound until she screamed, "Kill him now!"

As veins popped from her forehead, Victor gladly ran up to Orien, unsheathing his hatchet.

"Goodbye, insolent swine!" Victor said as he prepared to hack at him.

Just then, Orien rolled on his back, bursting out of his restraints and dodging Victor's hatchet. This allowed Orien to kick him in the groin and pummel him right in the jaw, leaving him unconscious. Through the many times Syric and Orien had been roughly imprisoned, Orien figured out a nifty trick. He could cut rope with his unclipped fingernail.

As you can imagine, the dirty trick infuriated Ma'amela so much she snarled the orders, "Cut his legs off and kill him! Now!"

Orien picked up Victor's hatchet and cut Syric and Fuzen free as no more than twenty-five guards slowly closed in on the three of them. They were scared but ready to fight for their lives, though they definitely got their chance but not before a mob of Wikas came back. Hungry and unhappy with the amount of food they received, the Wikas screamed bloody murder.

"Weeee-hika! Wina lika wahh!" was what the leader screamed from the pit of his round tummy.

"Noo, you already got ya payment!" Ma'amela explained as if they did not understand English.

"Wee-hika! Wina lika wahh."

"You will not get more food." Despite her efforts, the Gaffmonkeys wanted more food. When they realized they were not getting more food, they flailed their primitive spears and began to attack.

The sheer numbers were three Wikas to one bandit. They were to surely overwhelm the goat-eyed bandits. When a Gaffmonkey's excitement proves too powerful, an onslaught of ankle biting, back biting, and the ear biting will ensue. As history continues to evolve, still, no man alive could ever be prepared to face that kind of fight.

In the midst of this "gang war," Orien, Syric, and Fuzen were lumped in the middle of a seemingly impossible situation. The fighting involved everyone except Koldiar, as he was able to successfully avoid being seen. He snuck behind Ma'amela as her attention was drawn toward her men being thoroughly maimed and mangled. Koldiar reached for the lantern placed next to her, slowly curling his dirty fingers around the handle.

"Uh…uh…ahh…um! Mum! A-a-a-h-h!"

One of the slaves holding Ma'amela's back saw him and panicked.

"What the…?" Ma'amela said, quickly grabbing the other end of the lantern.

The tug-of-war for the tail was difficult, especially when the opposing team had four extra teammates. Inevitably, their combined strength was too much for the lantern's handle, and when the final tug was made, the handle broke. At the same time, Ma'amela's grip loosened when a livid Gaffmonkey leapt on her back and bit her back fat roll. This allowed Koldiar to snatch the lantern back his way, claiming possession of the tail for himself.

Surrounded by bandits and Gaffmonkeys alike, life seemed to stand still with all their attention on him. Even though Koldiar whistled as loud as has he could, Echo never arrived.

"You gon give me that tail, boy. Do not make me have to kill you," Ma'amela said, inching closer, snapping tiny twigs with each girthy footstep.

Then out of the crowd of Ma'amela's crew, a bandit stole a dagger from another and joined Koldiar's side. It was Ismiellia coming to his aid, ready to fight tooth and nail with him. With a sword in one hand and a dagger in the other, Ismiellia handed Koldiar the stolen dagger.

"When I tell you to run, you ru—" she yelled before being cut off by a deafening boom!

Echo crashed down on the camp, obliterating everything in the process and abruptly stopping Ismiellia midsentence. If Echo's grandiose entrance had not blown everyone flat, her echoing roar would have done the job, two waves of her monstrous power that should scare death itself. Echo quickly morphed into her human form and sashayed through the quivering and unconscious bodies to find Koldiar.

"Come on, Koldiar, we have to leave!" Ismiellia said with dust in her lungs as she tried to help him to his feet.

"Wait, she is my friend, the one that wants the tail back," Koldiar said, holding the cold lantern close to his chest.

"Your friend is a dragon? No…no, you cannot give it back to her," she insisted.

"She can keep it guarded. She is the only one that can."

"No! It must be destroyed! My father is desperate. He will not stop until it is in his possession even if it has to be stolen again! Give it to me so I can destroy it!" she yelled, trying to snatch the lantern. "If your father refuses to stop, then I will stop him myself.

Koldiar, give me the tail now."

With an icy response from Echo, she approached Koldiar from behind.

There was nowhere for Koldiar to run or to hide nor magic to give him a moment to think. He was trapped by Echo and Ismiellia's stubborn resolve breathing down his neck.

What do I do? he thought. However, it only took a moment for the decision to become obvious. He took the lantern and handed it to her willingly. The shock of betrayal stunned the other woman's heart. Echo was appalled.

Koldiar is a simple man, but to be a holy knight, he must do the right thing for Wallacgrum.

"I am sorry, Echo, but I have to follow the crown's order and make sure the king is protected even if it is from himself," he said, not knowing the treachery that was about to transpire.

Just before Echo was about to take the tail by force, a woman was heard singing from the middle of the camp. They all heard this ethereal voice lulling the masses with a mysterious song that could have only been heard from Echo's nightmares.

My pain will repeat itself.
My mistakes are completely mine.
We are doomed to never learn.
My sacrifice will echo throughout time.

This song from the golden box hushed the whole procession asleep apart from the three men responsible. Orien, Fuzen, and Syric all caused this happening and avoided its penalties by plugging their ears with the fur of a few Gaffmonkeys. No matter how vomitous that might have been, it was all according to plan to take advantage of the golden opportunity to steal the lantern back.

"I swear rigor mortis set in! She is not letting go!" said Syric, struggling to break the lantern free from Ismiellia's unconscious clutch.

"Oh, she is giving it up!" said the determined Orien, struggling to slide the lantern out from between Ismiellia's fingertips.

"Aye, wizard, get your things. We are leaving! Syric, take this and grab a carriage. Wizard, come on, what are you doing?'

"Taking Koldiar with us."

"If you touch him, he will wake up, and then we will have to split the reward four ways. Leave him."

"He saved our lives. He saved your life! We cannot just leave him."

"Ugh! Fine, bring him, but I am charging you a fee! Now hurry up, Syric should be ready, and grab that roasted pig too."

As you can expect through this journey, Koldiar had gotten used to the random blackout here and there and was not fazed when he woke up to Fuzen. The only question he had on his mind was if Echo were okay, but before he could wake her up, Fuzen stopped him before he did.

"Come now, Koldiar, we have the tail. We can go get our reward."

"Fuzen, the tail is too dangerous. If Ismiellia has gone this far to destroy it, it should not reach the king."

"Aarrgghh! Syric!"

"What happened?" Fuzen asked Orien, seemingly irate at the

moment.

"He took it and left! The little imp took the tail and left!" "What! There should be extra horses. We could use them to

catch up to him," Fuzen suggested.

"He set them all free before he left."

"Okay, I have an idea, but you will have to let me handle it," said Koldiar, dreading what he had to do next.

He had to wake Echo up and ask for a ride. He looked at her wonderfully peaceful face, knowing that all hell would break loose the moment he was to wake her. This time, he had to awaken the sleeping dragon. He sat on his feet and held her neck and caressed her tender cheek.

"Wake up, Echo. We need you to wake up."

Echo melted his heart when she fluttered her eyes open and gazed up at him. To be honest, she was ill-prepared to see the striking expression of concern and tenderness upon his dirty face.

"Koldiar," she replied with an innocent pout.

This would have been such a pleasant moment had not Koldiar ruined it with his poor news.

"Echo"—he gulped—"we need your help." Again he gulped. "Your tail is gone."

When the utterance of these words left Koldiar's mouth, a slight indentation formed between her brows as she scrunched her face in confused agitation.

"What do you mean? What—what happened? Where is it!" she echoed, looking around frantically.

"Well, what had happened was—" Koldiar tried to explain before Orien butted in.

"What had happened was, this ungrateful gnome stole my t—I mean your tail and is delivering your property to the king!"

"Who are you again?" Echo said as her eyes were glowing bluer and more intimidating.

"My name is O—"

"Never mind, I care not! What way is this gnome going?" "Um, uh, east?"

"Was that a question or a statement?" "E-East!"

She transformed, and with all the force in her wings, she flew off without any regard. Koldiar, Orien, and Fuzen stood there, not knowing what to do until Fuzen realized Ismiellia was lying unconscious beside Koldiar.

"Is that Ismiellia!" Fuzen said, rushing to wake her from her premature slumber. "Wake up! Ismiellia, wake up!" He was roughly shaking her.

She woke up, groggy and disorientated, and asked, "Mister Waykin?"

"Princess, what are you doing out here?"

"I was trying to stop my father from releasing whatever evil that is within that tail. I was so close to destroying the tail. That dragon woman probably used her trickery soul magic to steal it back. I suppose that in any case, the tail is somewhat protected from Father."

"Um, well, about that… Me, Koldiar, and a couple of other men were attempting to retrieve the tail for your father."

"Mister Waykin," she said, highly disappointed.

"Somewhere between him giving you the tail and now, one of our men decided to run off, taking the tail for himself," Fuzen confessed.

"For all my efforts, he will still—no! Mister Waykin, I need you to send me home!"

"That is not a good idea…"

"I know what you are going through, but I am going to need for you to believe you can and try."

"Very well, but I shall share the danger of my magic and go with you," he said, nervously clasping the trim of his robe.

"Orien, Koldiar, I am taking Ismiellia back home. I am afraid this is where we part ways."

"So you can hog the reward for bringing her back? Nah! I went through too much. I am getting some kind of reward!" Orien boorishly insinuated.

He and Fuzen had a brief back-and-forth of moral alignment of why each of them wanted to help the "rich white lady" before he reluctantly agreed to bring him.

"I want to go too," Koldiar begged hesitantly.

But Ismiellia interrupted before Fuzen's allowance with disapproval, "Koldiar, I know you want to help, but I cannot let you come. Your presence in the kingdom will only excite panic! Besides, I assume two of you is enough protection."

"But Princess—" Fuzen pried.

"Mr. Fuzen, this is my commanding order."

"Hmm, sorry, kid, but it seems I have no choice, and time is of the essence."

"Hmm, money…" was all Orien could say as he brushed past him, genuinely feeling bad for leaving him but not bad enough to stay.

"Besides, you can go back home now," Fuzen suggested.

Shockingly enough, Fuzen was able to successfully conjure a portal by casting "Aye Yee Fum." When they left, the words "go back home" felt more like an insult than an option. Honestly, how could he? He knew he made the wrong choice, but then again, neither one of the choices could have been right. While he slinked past all the sleeping Gaffmonkeys and unconscious bandits, he thought to himself, what if I just say sorry to her? No, no, she hates me now. Ugh, what do I do!

It was not long before he was miles down the sandy dirt road, still asking himself what to do, when he saw the sparkle of a small diamond in his path veering off to a small pond. The thought of what this would lead him to never crossed his mind, but he continued to follow all the same. His main thought was, I am a bit thirsty. To his surprise, he saw the trail of diamonds leading to a very miserable Echo. Koldiar's heart sputtered, the same way it did when he first laid eyes on her. When she noticed him, she turned away to hide her shame and piece her emotions back together.

"Echo? Are you okay? I thought you were searching for Syric?"

"Oh, I found him!" she said, tossing over a stump of wood. "It

was an illusion. I do not know where to go from here."

In Koldiar's mind, he now knew what he had to do, what he wanted to do, and what he had to do as this soon would be the only important thing in his life.

"Let me help you," he asked.

"I think you have done enough."

"I promise I will never betray you again. To make it up to you, I swear I will protect you at all costs, and I will show you the way."

Such tender words, which melted through Echo's callused exterior, blossomed a smile.

"Okay," she said gently.

"But we need to get there fast. So, may I?" Koldiar asked fearfully. "Fine, but just this once," Echo agreed.

Koldiar felt the scorching flames swirling around Echo as she then transformed into the magnificent crystal dragon that his dreams once fixated on. She stretched her wings and roared with a mighty echo. Echo seemed almost like a new woman driven by a new kind of power, something almost on the lines of love. However, Echo being Echo, she playfully shook Koldiar off her leg as he tried to climb.

"I told you I am not a mount!" She laughed.

"So then how is this going to work?" asked Koldiar.

She quickly grabbed Koldiar with her large talons and took off. She was gentle enough not to harm him but rough enough for him to loath their little arrangement. Even though Koldiar had a strong nauseous feeling welling in his stomach and a newly found fear of heights, he did not complain because he found that Echo's warmth soothed better than any hunting ointment he had ever made. More importantly, Koldiar was finally doing what he wanted and what felt right.

CHAPTER 16

Rotten Core

The last time we saw Ismiellia, Fuzen, and Orien, they entered a magical portal, leaving Koldiar alone. Unfortunately, the portal did not bring them as close to the castle as they may have hoped. They ended up landing six miles from the city walls and another few miles from the castle. The agitated princess did not waste any time making her way there, periodically jogging between her fast-paced walking. Fuzen did not mind the exercise too much; though he may have been old, he was fairly fit enough to keep up. Orien, on the other hand, was not thrilled with the whole "fast pace" part of their hike. He frequently refused to move any faster than he was usually inclined.

"Please, Mr. Fuzen, can you tell your friend to hurry up?"

"Not a problem, ma'am." Fuzen turned around to see Orien incredibly lagging.

"Hey, hoghead! Your princess demands you to hurry up!" "Ragging, fragging, brown-nosing—oh, don't fall asleep, wizard!" Orien mumbled to himself.

Nonetheless, he forced himself to catch up to Ismiellia and Fuzen. When they arrived at a royal roadblock entering the city of Wallacgrum, they saw a familiar gnome who just barely passed through its gates. It was Syric, looking incredibly pleased with himself with a grin so annoying that it lit a fire inside Orien.

"This is perfect. We can use the guards to bring him back!" said Fuzen.

"No, we cannot. They might be possessed by the tail," said Ismiellia.

"You believe the tail to be that foul?" asked Fuzen.

"I know it is. I was thrown in the dungeon because my guards were possessed."

"Well then, what would you have us do, Princess?" asked Fuzen. "Listen here, you and I will distract them while she sneaks through. That way we can pop the trunk on that two-timing mutant!"

said Orien.

"Pop the trunk?" asked Ismiellia.

"It means he plans to maim the gnome," said Fuzen, clarifying Orien's jargon yet again.

"Uh, all right. Well then, your plan will have to work for now," said Ismiellia.

"Just wait for the signal," Orien said before rushing down.

The plan started smoothly with Orien taking the lead and Fuzen trailing behind until, "Halt! Identify yourself and empty your pockets!"

"We are complying! We are complying!" Orien yelled, dropping to his knees with his hands up. "Wizard, get on your knees and put your hands behind your head," he whispered.

"What?" Fuzen asked.

"Get on your knees and put your hands behind your head. Just go with it."

At this point, the guards were very puzzled.

"Sir, sir, you do not have to—you are not under arrest. All we need is your name and to see what you are holding."

"We are innocent, officer!" said Orien.

"He made me do it!" said Fuzen, playing along.

"I was just having dinner!" Orien continued as one of the guards walked over to aid him to his feet.

"Sir, calm down and—" But when the guard touched him, Orien started convulsing. Violently shaking, Orien was on the ground kicking up dirt, laughing hysterically, and foaming at the mouth.

"What did you do!? He is going mad! You must help him! Help! Help! Help!" yelled Fuzen.

All the guards were distracted enough to leave their post to see what was going on. Apparently, that act of buffoonery was the signal, which gave Ismiellia enough time to sneak by. In hindsight, this ruse was probably in poor taste for a princess.

When Orien peeked out of his left eye to see that Ismiellia had made it through, his "mad fit" abruptly came to a halt. He jumped to his feet and gave all the information they needed.

"My name is Orien Alexander Fike, and this is my colleague Fuzen Waykin. In our possession, we currently have one staff, a war hammer, thirty diamonds, a bottle of wine, and two moldy pies."

"Um, okay, I still have to check you to make sure you're not carrying any contraband."

The guards were still fairly stunned; they did not have the right set of rules for what just happened.

"I suppose everything checks out. You can go," the searching guard said, clearing them to walk through the threshold of the city.

"Wait! Say your business here again?" the other guard asked. For most people, a follow-up question would freak them out,

but not Orien; he quickly responded with, "Medical help." "Oh…oh well, carry on. I hope it works out, sir," said the confused guard, trying to avoid eye contact.

Orien and Fuzen then nonchalantly blended in with the rest of the city folk and connected back with Ismiellia.

"That was amazing!" said Ismiellia. "Works every time," said Orien.

"You were so great!" said Ismiellia, clutching Fuzen's arm. "That was embarrassing. I cannot believe I did that. Hold on, you do that often, and how did you make your mouth foam?" questioned Fuzen.

"You better believe I do, wizard. That is too good of a ruse to not have on rotation! And the secret to foaming at the mouth is bone salt," Orien said, immensely proud of himself.

"But bone salt is actually poisonous!"

"Well, that is why I foam at the mouth, buckethead!"

"Hm…all right, I am going to let it go," Fuzen replied. "Besides, wizard, you did good. You might actually be useful after all."

For a short moment, they celebrated their small victory, but as great as it was, it was short-lived. Ismiellia started to feel anxious and paranoid, and she felt as though she was being watched. Ismiellia forced herself to stay calm and thought to herself, Nobody knows who I am. I am fine. My face is covered. We will be fine.

Even though her face was covered and nobody should have known who she was, a poor beggar man was standing at attention, and Ismiellia noticed him staring her down in the middle of the dusty alley. Their eyes met only for a moment, but she looked away before the whites of his eyes blackened.

The further into the city they walked, the more Ismiellia became uneasy. She came to find out she was not the only one feeling uncomfortable; Orien and Fuzen felt as if they stuck out like two flaming buffalo rats.

As they were walking, a woman courted Ismiellia's attention. "Excuse me, excuse me, ma'am. You dropped something."

Ismiellia turned around to see an innocent woman with a pleasant smile on her face, almost easing the wound tension of anxiety she developed. However, her sweet face quickly turned to crazed anger as she snatched the bandage wraps from around Ismiellia's face.

The crazed woman's eyes turned black as she yelled, "She is here! The princess is here!"

Then townspeople's eyes rapidly started turning black as they began to walk closer. Orien suddenly kicked the woman in the chest, knocking her back as Fuzen grabbed Ismiellia's arm and started to run.

"Orien! You just kicked that woman in the chest!" said Ismiellia as they ran for their lives.

"I believe in equal rights when witchcraft is involved! So excuse me for saving your life!"

Every two out of three people they passed suddenly dropped whatever they were doing just to chase after them. They had hoped that if they could just reach the castle gates, they would be safe. On the bright side, they were able to run fast enough to lose the big crowd of seemingly possessed people. On the bad side, they had not gotten any closer to the castle than when they were initially chased.

"Now do you believe me?" Ismiellia asked, trying to catch her breath."

"It seems as though there may be a bit of validity to your story," Orien replied, also panting heavily.

"Now that we know what we are dealing with, we should stay out of sight," said Fuzen.

"Hold on now. I am the one making the plans," Orien said, pausing for a moment to think. Then he continued, "Now that we know what we are dealing with, we should stay out of sight."

"I do not know just yet," Fuzen said.

"Hmm, we could…no, that is a bad idea," Ismiellia said to herself.

"What is it, Princess?"

"Hmm, we could take the royal escape tunnels. But I cannot stress this enough, neither one of you can ever use the tunnels or tell anyone where they are."

"Well, it depends on what is more important for you—these tunnels or your father's safety?" said Fuzen.

In a moment of thought, Ismiellia could hear the riffraff of the crazed mob closing in on them.

"Princess!" Orien shouted, and this only solidified her decision. "Fine. Follow me!"

She led them to a fountain statue of the late Queen Mara Fayos pouring an overflowing jug.

"That is a fine woman," Orien said, staring at the soft-featured woman made of marble.

Fuzen elbowed him. "That is her mother," he said under his breath.

"Not only was my mother beautiful, but she was also a generous woman who gave more than she took, even if it was her own life," she said, pushing the vase that the statue held upward.

This stopped the pouring of water and drained the pool through the passageway as it rasped open, revealing a spiral staircase before them.

"I am trusting the both of you. Please keep this to yourselves."
"You have our word, Princess!"

"Don't speak for me, wizard! But yes, your secret is safe," Orien said, already thinking of how he was going to exploit these tunnels. They followed Ismiellia down the leaky entrance and into a pitch-black tunnel. She grabbed a Ta'un glow torch that hung on the wall and then struck the floor with its red gem tip that activated its glow. From there, Ismiellia traversed those tunnels as if she lived there. She was swift as she avoided several boobytraps and pitfalls with ease. Orien and Fuzen were on their toes the whole time, while Ismiellia casually conversed as they fumblingly jogged behind her.

Finally, after practically sprinting on and off, avoiding traps, they arrived at a staircase leading them to the center of the royal courtyard. The grassy disguised hatch was swung open, and Ismiellia, Fuzen, and Orien emerged. Luckily for them, the guards that patroled this particular area had already just passed by.

"Hush! This way," she said.

She then led them through the private dining hall into the kitchen and out through the service doors leading to the grand hall throne room.

When they burst through the doors, they saw Syric being escorted by Thespis to King Fayos. "Father, stop!" cried Ismiellia.

"Now where have you been? We have been looking everywhere for you. I am so pleased you are here!" King Fayos exclaimed.

"It is okay, Father. I am here now, but I need to—" she said, clasping his arm, only realizing he was not speaking to her but to the tail in Syric's hands.

"All of Wallacgrum thanks you for what you have done." "Father, you cannot take this tail!" she was saying when out of nowhere King Fayos struck her face with the back of his hand. Orien and Fuzen instinctively came to her rescue, forgetting who the king was for a moment.

"How dare you tell me what I can and cannot do! Not only am I your father, but I am your king. You will treat me as such and trust my judgment! Guards, seize her," he shouted while waving over two royal guards to guide and detain Princess Ismiellia to her room.

"How could you treat your daughter like that!" Fuzen yelled, forgetting himself and whom he was speaking to.

"Hmm, Mr. Fuzen, you came too? Guards, seize him and his friend as well."

"Really, Father, you are that far gone?" Ismiellia gently said, concealing her scarred cheek as her heart quickly shattered.

"I apologize for the interruptions, young Syric. How can Wallacgrum ever repay you?" he said, turning around to face Syric again.

"Well, Your Majesty, I would like to be tall," Syric said, handing over the lantern.

However, as Syric waited for his reply, the king seemed almost hypnotized by the blue flames.

"Your Majesty?"

King Fayos paused for a moment, completely entranced by the tail.

When the pause slightly broke, he gave the order, "Ah yes, yes. Guard, put him with the others too," he said before snuffing out the blue flames and snatching out the blackened tail within. The sound of the lantern glass breaking felt wrong to all when it hit the floor. "What! You gon' be like that?" Syric said while being escorted away, just like the rest were.

However, as Syric left, Thespis slithered to the King's side. "Yes, thou hath done it, my liege. Now consume it! Take your

power back!" he whispered in his ear.

King Fayos took the advice and ravenously devoured the tail. This crazed king ripped and snorted as he ate, and when finished, his body began to mutate. He fell to the floor in excruciating pain. Echo and Koldiar then crashed through the glass ceiling above them, landing in front of King Fayos. They arrived just in time to watch as two horns erupted from his forehead and two black wings sprouted from his back side. From where there was none, now it donned a tail.

King Fayos was not King Fayos anymore; he was someone else, or rather, something else. He picked himself up and glared at Echo with blackened eyes that made her physically ill.

"What…what have you done?" Echo shuddered. "Echo, my dear tail of old, did you miss me?"

For that time of terror, Echo realized she had not been referred to by that title in centuries.

It knocked the wind out of her lungs as she whispered, "Obsidian? No, you died."

"No! Echo, I am very much still alive. All my soul needed was a body," he said, slowly walking to her with black haze leaking from his mouth.

"This cannot be happening… This is not happening…," she said, backing away from the terrible being possessing King Fayos.

She felt overwhelmed as the black smoke formed into the dragon Obsidian once was, towering over her, terrorizing her into submission. Echo painfully tried to roar, but her once mighty echoing roar now sounded more pathetic than intimidating.

"Yes, this is happening. This is happening because of you, because of all your sins!" he now yelled in a two-toned voice heard by hell.

Koldiar did not understand what was happening between the two dragons, but he knew Echo was in danger, and in that intense moment, he could hear the voice of his father urging him to believe in Jehovah's power. Then as a physical agreement, faith finally grew in this man, and he stood in front of Echo with his arms spread open, defending her.

"Back away from her!" Koldiar yelled.

"How sweet. You want to protect her? Let us see if you can!" Obsidian said before channeling all of his darkness into a deadly spear.

Even though Obsidian summoned immense power, Koldiar stood his ground against him with feet strongly planted to guard her. However, in his head, there was a swirling slew of panic and fear. His resolve to protect Echo kept him sturdy, but he needed more; he needed power.

In his mind, Koldiar prayed, I now understand what you want from me to access your strength! I will have faith!

Just before Obsidian's attack could touch Koldiar, a golden heater shield appeared in front of him—a five-foot-tall shield with the words "Now Faith Is" engraved in its honor point. This was the power he needed, the power granted by Jehovah; this was the shield of faith, the only thing that could have withstood the full brunt of Obsidian's continuous attack.

"Foolish human, give up! You have no business protecting her!" he said as his attack continued.

"Never! I made a promise to protect her!" Koldiar said, barely holding back the darkness.

"Ha! Did she not tell you? I was the first to protect her! And for all my efforts, she turned around and severed my tail just like this!"

Then out of the smoky tail of Obsidian's fake form, King Fayos appeared to slice off Echo's tail with a blade formed from his darkness. She roared in agony as he was able to cut past her crystal scales and straight through her bones. There is no worse feeling alive than for a dragon to lose their tail, and this was no exception. As the smoke dissipated, she, too, melted away her form. She was human, she was fetal, and she was lifeless.

The moment Obsidian ceased his attack, Koldiar saw him rising through the shattered pane ceiling using his demon-like wings to raise him higher. Obsidian achieved the first of many of his successions, and the second was his coronation that he did above his new kingdom.

"Now I am your king! And we are legion!" he said, hovering above them all.

From his mouth, black flames shot to the twilight sky, creating a city-sized sphere. When it exploded, ash fell like snow, turning Wallacgrum black.

Fortunately, Fuzen, Orien, and Ismiellia were able to break free with the help of the sneaky gnome, Syric. He knocked the two distracted guards to their knees and allowed Orien and Ismiellia to finish them off. When Orien realized it was Syric, he was both angry and relieved.

"Look who came crawling back!" he said.

"This is not the time, Orien!" Fuzen shouted as he continued to cast a spell. "Lou ta e fu mi ta!"

This spell formed a temporary barrier of sealing around Obsidian and a barrier of protection around Fuzen and his allies, although it did not take long for Obsidian to notice Fuzen's magic and use all his might to break out. He cracked Fuzen's most powerful barrier little by little with each attempt.

"Koldiar! Come this way! We have to go now!" Fuzen yelled before seeing his daughter, Elizabeth Waykin, walk out of the royal service kitchen doors.

"Father?" Elizabeth said, looking around at all the chaos that befell the room. "What is going on here?"

"Elizabeth! Come here!" Fuzen said, pulling her close and firmly hugging her. "We must leave the city. I will explain later."

Meanwhile, Koldiar dropped to his knees near Echo; he would not leave if it meant leaving her.

"Echo, Echo, please wake up!" he said and bent over, holding her head.

There seemed to be no response, but with their skin connected and a simple kiss, Koldiar gave Echo half of his life. Fully connected to Koldiar, she was able to take a shallow breath. Although she was not fully awake yet, she was breathing, and that was all Koldiar needed to know before carrying her out of the castle.

"This way, everyone!" shouted Fuzen, guiding everyone through the castle and to the tunnel hatch.

When everyone made it into the trapdoor, Fuzen decided to stay out. He refused to let his daughter be subject to that false king.

"Fuzen, what are you doing!?" pleaded Koldiar. "Stop playing, wizard!" said Orien.

"Please, Father!" begged Elizabeth. "Come on, don't be stupid!" yelled Syric. "Mr. Waykin," said Ismiellia.

"The spell only holds if I stay close to the thing I want to seal. I must protect my friends, and most of all, I will protect my daughter! Take care, sweetheart. I love you."

With bitter farewells, Fuzen kissed his daughter's forehead and forced the grassy hatch closed.

Obsidian took sight of all this but was not furious Echo escaped; he was surprisingly happy she did. In fact, he was more excited for the hunt than her death. Therefore, he let them run as he took Fuzen prisoner. Ismiellia led them all through the royal tunnels to escape the city. As they ran through the tunnels, Obsidian declined to let Echo leave without a few discouraging words that took control of the darkness with the power of his voice—words that would haunt her every time she saw a shadow.

"I hope you see now that I will never die! I am the endless nightmare you will never wake from. I am the hopelessness you hopelessly cling to. I am the lump that chokes you as you weep. I am the scratch marks you leave as I speak. Heed my words, Blood! I promise to ruin you with every ounce of blood I obtain. I am your sins! I am your consequence! I am Obsidian, Tail of Young, the dragon of the rotten flame, and your tail is now mine!"

Our blood is now water.
The only thing that died all
those years ago
was my love for you.

—Obsidian

About *the* Author

Hear ye! Introducing Khanyon G. Jerome, the proud author of *Echo's Tale: Burden of the Tail* and late nineties baby with a passion for more. Khanyon's combined enthusiasm for emotional films and elaborate stage productions like Hamilton, books, video games, and his favorite activity Dungeons and Dragons have all led him to this fascinating piece of literature. Inspired by renaissance and fantasy, Khanyon's hobbies include fencing and playing the piano. He also loves lavish meals like pheasant under glass, but don't omit simple pleasures like ale and fried chicken. Khanyon enjoys sharing his home-cooked masterpieces and his free time with his family who inspired some of the characters in this story. Always marching to the beat of his own drum, Khanyon's family was not surprised by his determination to produce Echo's Tail, a unique story that highlights Black characters surrounded by pixies, trolls, elves, and dragons within the fantasy realm.

Khanyon G. Jerome is the self-proclaimed Lion Scribe of Southern California's Inland Empire. As long as he can remember, the 28 years old has had an affinity for emotional and dramatic films, plays, books, and video games set in the fantasy genre. Much of his influence has come from stories like Hunchback of Notre Dame, Hamilton, The most Dangerous Game, as well as the Kingdom Hearts series. In addition,

Khanyon loves spending time in the kitchen creating his own recipes and spicing up pre-written recipes. His willingness to experiment combined with ambition and creativity are qualities instilled by his parents Arthur Garey and Dr. Pamela Garey.

As a jack of all trades, he has been blessed with opportunities like participating in the Junior Olympics as a fencer, learning to play the piano, and even performing maintenance on wind turbines. All of these experiences have led him to where he is now. If it were not for God guiding his path, the Echo's Tale series would not be in existence.

Khanyon is proud of his support system from his wife, Fawna Garey, to his parents, sister, and close friends whom he also considers family. They have been his driving force and have encouraged him to walk the path least traveled. As Khanyon starts the new year joining the She Publishing family, he also anticipates the arrival of the newest member of his own family. It goes without saying that 2024 will be the best year yet!

ECHO'S TALE

9 781964 061078